Love Waits

D1014289

GERRI HILL

Bella
BOOKS
2010

Bella Books, Inc.
P.O. Box 10543
Tallahassee, FL 32302

Printed in the United States of America on acid-free paper
First Edition

Editor: Anna Chinappi
Cover Designer: Linda Callaghan

ISBN 13:978-1-59493-186-4

About the Author

Gerri Hill has eighteen published works, including 2009 GCLS winner *Partners* and 2007 GCLS winners *Behind the Pine Curtain* and *The Killing Room*, as well as GCLS finalist *Hunter's Way* and Lambda finalist *In the Name of the Father*. She began writing lesbian romance as a way to amuse herself while snowed in one winter in the mountains of Colorado and hasn't looked back. Her first published work came in 2000 with *One Summer Night*. Hill's love of nature and of being outdoors usually makes its way into her stories as her characters often find themselves in beautiful natural settings. When she isn't writing, Hill and her longtime partner, Diane, can be found at their home in East Texas, where their vegetable garden, orchard and five acres of piney woods keep them busy. They share their lives with two Australian Shepherds and an assortment of furry felines. For more, see her website: www.gerrihill.com.

CHAPTER ONE

Gina Granbury rested her chin in her palm, her eyes scanning the drawing she'd been tinkering with for the last two hours. Their deadline was approaching but there were only so many ways to advertise pre-owned cars. She dropped her pencil and shoved the drawing away in frustration.

"Why don't you let Darrell give it a try?"

Gina shot a wry glance at Tracy, her business partner. "Because he uses a computer for all of his designs, that's why."

"So do you."

"Not until I have my ideas down with pencil first," she said as she leaned back with a sigh. "These college kids nowadays, they don't have to have an original thought. They just copy and paste images and then call it good."

Tracy laughed. "You're only cranky because you hate car ads. You always have. Why did you take on this account in the first place?"

"Oh? So you think we're thriving enough that we can be selective in our choices?" Gina stood and held up her coffee cup in a silent question. Tracy shook her head.

"Business has been fabulous, and you know it. And since it's you who hates car ads—yet you took on this one—why don't you just give it to Darrell and let him do his computer thing and call it good?"

"Because I'm stubborn."

"And it has nothing to do with the deal he gave you on your new Jeep?"

Gina childishly stuck her tongue out at Tracy, then slipped into the tiny corner kitchen, suspiciously eyeing the coffee that had been brewed some five hours earlier. Her semi-addiction to coffee had its limits. She took a water bottle from the fridge instead. Leaning against the counter, she gazed out through the kitchen door opening to the office. They'd started their agency six years ago, building it up ever so slowly. The first two years had been lean and they'd talked about quitting, yet they hung on. Their big break came when a new restaurant opened up in their small city. A young couple with a dream of duplicating their parents' authentic Mexican food recipes—they couldn't afford one of the larger, more established advertising agencies. Antonio and Norma had come in off the street and pitched their idea to them. The couple wanted to serve delicious, authentic food in an atmosphere that was fun and vibrant. Gina and Tracy had worked nonstop for months, coming up with print and radio ads, each one fresh and original—and enticing. They had to be. There was a Mexican food restaurant on every block. She'd come up with the catch phrase about two a.m. one morning when sleep eluded her. *Is your old Mexican food place holding you like a ball and chain? Don't let it weigh you down. If you really want to have a ball, bounce over to Antonio's Café and Cantina, where the fun never stops!*

She smiled and shook her head. It was as corny as hell, but Antonio and Norma loved it. Apparently, so did the public. The place had been jam-packed on opening night, and like the ads promised, the fun hadn't stopped yet.

The same was true for their business. After that successful campaign, more and more of the local businesses started coming their way. So much so that they'd been forced to hire another designer—Darrell. That freed up Tracy to use her marketing skills for their own business, soliciting new accounts while Gina and Darrell designed the ads. The new strategy was paying off. Tracy was bringing in so many new accounts, they'd actually talked about hiring a fourth person.

The slamming of the front door brought her out of her musings and she pushed off the counter, going to see what had Darrell so animated.

"Gorgeous, I tell you. He was absolutely *gorgeous*." Darrell spun around, smiling brilliantly at Gina. "Yes, I'm in love."

"Again?" she asked dryly.

He put one hand on his hip, dramatically arching it in her direction as he looked down his nose at her. "At least one of us is not afraid of love," he said.

She ignored his comment as she went back to her desk. "You better be careful, Darrell. This city is not that large. You're going to run out of boys to date pretty soon." She picked up the car ad and handed it to him. "Do something with this, will you?"

"Used car dealership? How boring."

"Pre-owned," she corrected.

"Oh, yes. That makes *all* the difference." He shoved the day's stack of mail at her. "Your turn to sort."

She waved the mail at Tracy. "Isn't it your turn?"

Tracy held out her hand. "Give it here. I swear, you two act like it's a chore to sort the mail. Either it's a bill or a check, or it's junk." She pulled out a bright green envelope and held it up. "This is addressed to you."

Even though Gina lived in the apartment above their office space, she rarely got mail. She was strictly online and paperless. She took the green envelope and stared at it, the return address bringing in a flood of memories. She turned it over in her hands, then nervously tucked her dark hair behind her ears before breaking the seal.

CHAPTER TWO

Twenty-four years earlier

Gina dribbled the basketball blindly, her eyes never leaving the cheerleaders as they practiced on the other side of the gym. She pretended to eye them all, but it was only Ashleigh Pence who held her interest.

"Yo, Gina. You going to pass the ball or what?"

Embarrassed, she turned, firing a one-handed bullet at LaQuita, nearly knocking her down from the force. "I'm going to pass the ball, of course," she said as she jogged past her.

The whistle blew and she stopped dead in her tracks, waiting for Coach Beam to yell at her.

"Gina! I don't care if you are our top scorer. You sit your butt on the bench the rest of practice. I won't have showboating."

Gina sulked as she walked over to the bench, wishing she could keep her mind on basketball—her one love—instead of Ashleigh Pence. Even now she found her eyes straying across the gym, picking Ashleigh out of the group of nearly identical looking skinny blond girls.

Having gone to Catholic school through the eighth grade, she'd never laid eyes on the girl before. Now that they were at the same high school, she found herself running into her constantly, each time more distressing to her. Her hormones were alive and kicking but instead of directing her to boys, they led her directly to Ashleigh Pence. She rolled her eyes. A *cheerleader*, for God's sake. A *popular* skinny blond cheerleader. And Gina was all legs and arms, having grown five inches over the summer, all the while working on her basketball skills, knowing a scholarship was the only way she'd get to a university. Her folks had told her if she didn't get a scholarship, she'd be going to a community college instead.

So with hormones raging, she avoided the boys, most shorter than her anyway, and she avoided the popular girls, already knowing at this young age where her preference was. She tried to fade into the background as much as possible, never wanting anyone to know her secret. However, making the varsity team as a freshman wasn't exactly the way to avoid notice.

But making the varsity team had its perks. The cheerleaders went to every game, home and away.

She flicked her eyes again across the gym, her heart stopping completely as Ashleigh Pence stared back at her, her gaze as intense as Gina's.

CHAPTER THREE

Present Day

"Earth to Gina. Hello?"

Gina looked up, blinking several times, trying to focus on Tracy. "What?"

"I said, who is it from? You're as white as a sheet."

Gina turned away, dropping the envelope and accompanying invitation on her desk. "It just...took me back is all. Twenty-year high school reunion," she said.

"Twenty? Good Lord, how old are you?"

Gina picked up the stress ball she kept on her desk, tossing it at Tracy who caught it expertly. "I'm the same age as you are."

"God, are we that old? Twenty years out of high school?"

"Afraid so."

"Well, are you going?"

Gina shook her head. "No." She shrugged. "I haven't seen any of those people since the day we graduated."

"I know. I think that's the point. You go to catch up and see who's made a success out of themselves and who let themselves turn into old, fat, frumpy married women."

Gina laughed. "And you would fall into the latter category," she teased. She caught the stress ball without looking as Tracy tossed it back at her in mock anger.

"I'm not fat. And married with two kids does not make me old and frumpy."

"No. But your poofy hairdo and your insistence on wearing those formal business suits do."

"So I should dress like you? Shorts and flip-flops?" She eyed Gina's attire with just a hint of envy. "There are certain rules one has to follow in the business world, Gina, even if we do live in a coastal town. I am the face of our little company when I am out and about mingling with the money shakers of this city."

"And you do it very well." Gina tossed the ball back at her. "I also know you love it."

Tracy grinned. "Yes, I do." She squeezed the stress ball between her hands, her perfectly manicured nails grazing the surface. "So, this high school reunion thing. Why won't you go? It could be loads of fun. You haven't been back to your hometown in forever, have you?"

Gina pulled her chair closer to Tracy's desk, then slouched down in it, her long bare legs stretched out in front of her. *Dare she even consider going back?*

"You remember back in college when we first met?"

"Of course."

"I was dating a girl from high school."

"Oh, yes. Your first love. What was her name?"

Gina swallowed. "Ashleigh. Ashleigh Pence."

"That's right. But you broke up with her, didn't you?" Tracy leaned closer. "That's when you turned into a whore dog, right?"

Gina narrowed her eyes. "I hate when you call me that."

"Yes, the truth hurts."

Yes, it did. She looked away. "It would be weird, that's all. You know, to see her again."

7

"Gina, sweetie, that's twenty years of water under the bridge. That's the point of going back to these things. To reminisce and to see these people you dated in high school. And then to be so thankful you didn't settle down with one of them. Trust me, these high school reunions are what make you appreciate your current life." Tracy tossed the ball back at her. "I went to my tenth reunion. The guy I was madly in love with was there with his wife. He was mostly bald and had a beer gut. His wife was eight months pregnant and looked like she worked as a prison guard." Tracy wrinkled up her nose. "Gross. To think I wanted to marry that guy." She grinned. "That night, Sammy and I had the best sex in years."

"I coulda gone without hearing that."

"I'm just saying."

"I know. And I may decide to go. It would be a good excuse to see Aunt Lou again."

Actually, she hadn't seen Aunt Lou since her father's funeral six years ago. And she hadn't been back to Calloway since the day she'd left for college. To her surprise, her parents had sold their house and moved to San Antonio that fall. And more shockingly, they divorced a year later. She was angry at both of them and resented them terribly for not only selling her childhood home, but for breaking up the family. It was a chasm in their relationship that they never really got over. Of course, her mother's disapproval of her lifestyle didn't help either. Yes, she had finally accepted that Gina was gay, but no, she wasn't happy that her only child would never marry and give her grandchildren, a fact she reminded Gina of nearly every time they spoke, which wasn't often. Aunt Lou, on the other hand, had always been understanding and accepting. Even though they didn't see each other, they spoke on the phone frequently.

"Hey, Gina. What do you think?"

Gina turned her eyes to the large monitor that hung on the far wall. It was where they projected their designs, bouncing ideas off each other. Darrell had whipped up the car dealership ad in record time, using an environmentally friendly theme—recycle, reuse—to urge potential car buyers to adopt these pre-owned beauties instead of buying new.

"It's perfect."

"Maybe we can get him to hang a *Go Green* sign in his lot."

"Somehow I don't picture Bubba Clarkston as a *Go Green* type of guy."

Darrell grinned wickedly. "Then maybe I need to go over there and flirt with that cute son of his. Maybe I could persuade him."

"And maybe you'll get shot," Gina said, tossing the stress ball at Darrell.

He dropped it.

CHAPTER FOUR

Present Day

Ashleigh gasped for air as she struggled to keep pace with Pam. She hated running. She'd much rather be on a bike but running was Pam's passion. They met up every other day at the gym, then took one day a week for either biking or jogging, today being Pam's day.

Her friend finally slowed, taking it down to an easy jog, allowing Ashleigh to catch up. Ashleigh reached out an arm, tugging Pam to a stop. She bent over, hands on her knees as she sucked in air.

"It's psychological, you know."

"Shut up."

"You don't do this when we ride."

"Exactly my point," Ashleigh said as she straightened up, her breathing returning somewhat to normal. She pushed her hair off her face, tucking the stray strands behind her ears. Her hair was just barely long enough for a ponytail and she pulled it out now, shaking it loose.

"You're in excellent shape and you're not winded when we ride. That's why I'm saying it's psychological."

"The bicycle was invented for a reason."

"Yeah. For lazy people who didn't want to run."

"Well, let's be lazy and walk back to my apartment. I could use a cold drink."

"That was barely three miles."

Ashleigh shrugged. "It's getting too hot."

"Since when do we make excuses?"

Ashleigh laughed. "Let's start today."

She turned and headed back, knowing Pam would follow. The hike and bike trail was two blocks from her condo and they knew it like the back of their hands. On a good day, they'd make the loop once when running, twice when biking. Today wasn't a good day.

"Want to tell me what's bugging you? Bad day at work?"

"Every day's a bad day at work," she said.

"You have a cushy job and you make lots of money. How bad can it be?"

"I hate my job. I hate the people I work with. I hate dealing with oil and gas bigwigs. I hate all the bullshit politics that I have to deal with. I hate my job," she said again.

"You've hated your work since the day I met you. Why don't you get out?"

"Because corporate law is what I studied for, what I trained for...what I know. And you're right. I have a cushy job and make lots of money." She waved her hand dismissively. "That's not what's bothering me anyway."

"My second guess would be your love life, but since you're not dating—again—that can't be it."

"I haven't been in the mood to date. It's depressing. The older you get, the less there is to choose from."

"I have introduced you to some very nice, attractive, professional women in the last couple of years, so don't say it's depressing."

Ashleigh sighed. "I know you have. There's just never a spark. I want there to at least be a spark if I'm going to sleep with them."

"I've known you almost ten years, Ashleigh. I only recall you dating two women for any length of time. Two. And I really liked Sara. She was fun."

"Yes, she was fun. So much fun that she liked to date three or four women at once. No thanks. I don't care for sloppy seconds."

"So is that what's bothering you? That you're not dating?"

"No. What's bothering me is I have a high school reunion coming up and all of *them* will know I'm not dating. Again."

"Again?"

"I went to my tenth reunion. I wasn't dating anyone then, either."

"And this is what?"

"Twenty years."

"Oh, my God! How old are you?"

"You know very well how old I am."

Pam laughed. "Yeah. Two years older than me." She bumped her arm. "So don't go."

"I have to go. I was class president. I was Miss Calloway the year we graduated. And the damn prom queen. Besides, my mother would kill me if I didn't go. It's a small town. If I didn't go, everyone would talk and wonder why. My mother hates it when people talk." Ashleigh stopped. "That's not really what's bothering me either." She pulled Pam to the side of the trail as a group of bike riders sped past. "*She* might be there."

"She?"

"You know."

"I do?"

Ashleigh rolled her eyes.

"Oh. *That* she. The girl you lost your virginity to?"

"Gina Granbury." God, Ashleigh thought to herself, just saying her name brought back a rash of memories. Memories she'd tried so hard to repress over the years.

"And you think she'll be there?"

"She wasn't at the tenth, thank goodness. But twenty? Everyone goes to their twentieth reunion, don't they?"

"How long has it been since you've seen her?"

Ashleigh started walking again. "My first semester in college. I transferred. She was sleeping with practically every girl at school. It was disgusting."

"Is this the one who broke up with you without giving you a reason?"

"Yes."

"You were still in love with her?"

"Madly. But we were kids. What do kids know about love?"

CHAPTER FIVE

Twenty-three years earlier

Ashleigh hurried down the hall, not bothering to stop at her locker to dump off the books she didn't need. She smiled and waved at Crissy, another cheerleader, but didn't stop to chat. She knew Gina Granbury rode her bike to and from school, so she hurried out the side door where the bike racks were. For some reason, the tall, dark-haired girl intrigued her. She often felt her eyes on her, often caught her staring. There was just something about the way Gina Granbury looked at her. It was mysterious. It was also a little frightening. She didn't know Gina. Not really. They'd had a class together their freshman year but they rarely spoke. Now their sophomore year had all but passed and they'd only said a handful of "hellos" to each other. They had only one class together this year—American history—and they sat at opposite sides of the room. Even then, whenever she turned, she found Gina watching her. The other girl would look away, embarrassment showing on her face each time. This confused Ashleigh more than frightened her. Gina Granbury was obviously harmless. But the look in her eyes...well, it was almost like how a boy would look at a girl. *That* frightened her. Only a little.

There was a whirr of bikes and bodies as everyone raced away from school. She spotted Gina in the middle of the pack, her long dark hair flowing out behind her as she peddled away.

"Crap," she murmured. It was Friday. She wouldn't have a chance to see Gina again until Monday. She spun around, wondering what her mother would say if she suddenly started riding her bike to school each day. She would think she'd flipped out, of course. The *cool* kids didn't ride their bikes to school. The cool kids either drove themselves or, better yet, rode with a cute guy.

She walked back inside, slower now. She was a cheerleader. She was officially one of the *cool* kids. She couldn't ditch her new car for a bike. She'd waited too long to be able to drive to go back to bikes.

"Hey, Ashleigh. Wanna go swimming?"

Ashleigh stopped at her locker, her fingers moving automatically over the combination lock, turning it at precisely the correct spot. "Where?"

"Jennifer's house." Crissy leaned against the locker next to hers. "James will be there," she said, her sing-song voice teasing Ashleigh. Everyone knew James had the hots for her.

"Boys?"

"Yeah. Jennifer's mom said she was finally old enough to have unsupervised parties with boys." She rolled her eyes dramatically. "As if we weren't old enough last year."

Ashleigh took two books out of her backpack, then slammed her locker shut. "Yeah, she wouldn't allow it if she knew that Jennifer's been screwing Seth since last summer."

Crissy laughed. "Speaking of that, when are you going to give in and go out with James?"

Ashleigh shook her head. "I don't like James. Not like that."

"What's not to like? He's one of the cutest guys in school."

15

"There's just no spark there. I need there to be a spark," Ashleigh said, surprised that her mind flashed to Gina Granbury and those dark eyes that often watched her.

"Maybe if you'd go out with him, there'd be a spark," Crissy said, tugging at her arm as they walked down the nearly empty hallway.

Ashleigh shrugged. "I don't know. Maybe."

"Oh, and you know that basketball player? The one who made the varsity team last year as a freshman?"

Ashleigh stopped. "Gina Granbury?" she said, the name sounding strange to her and she realized it was the first time she'd spoken it out loud.

"Yeah, her. Jennifer invited her to the party, too."

"Why? Does she even know her?"

"Not really. But Brian thinks she's hot."

"Brian? But he's—"

"They broke up."

"When?" Ashleigh started walking again, her mind racing. Gina Granbury at the swim party? She didn't know whether she was happy or annoyed. Yes, she wanted to get to know her. She just didn't necessarily want the whole gang to get to know her.

"They had a fight last weekend. Cheri told him to go fuck himself," she said, breaking into a fit of giggles.

"He's an asshole."

"He's the quarterback. What do you expect?"

Ashleigh's mind wasn't on Brian. She chewed her lip as she wondered what she'd wear. Boys would be there. It stood to reason she'd wear her bikini. Then she imagined those dark eyes watching her and she felt an involuntary chill. Maybe she should wear the more conservative one-piece. She tilted her head thoughtfully, a slow smile forming.

Or maybe not.

Ashleigh pulled her long T-shirt off, conscious of the tiny bikini she wore. She expected wolf whistles from the guys and she wasn't disappointed. Pity not a one of them stirred any interest in her. She stood at the edge of the pool, then dove in, disappearing underwater, loving the cool, clean feel of the water on her heated skin. When she surfaced, she wasn't surprised to find Gina Granbury watching her. Gina pulled her eyes away immediately but not before Ashleigh felt the heat of them.

Again, she didn't understand the pull, didn't understand her fascination with Gina. They weren't friends. They never ran into each other outside of school. In fact, she doubted anyone at the party had ever spent time with Gina. Yet here she was, at their swim party because Brian The Asshole thought Gina was hot. She'd seen Brian talk to her, had seen the other girl smile at him, but Gina still sat alone, removed from the others, her red one-piece suit revealing little, other than she had a perfect athlete's body.

Ashleigh lifted herself out of the pool, pausing as her thoughts sunk home. Gina was *invited* because Brian thought she was hot. But that wasn't the reason Gina was here. No, Gina was here because Ashleigh was here. She turned slowly, again finding Gina's eyes on her. This time, she didn't look away as quickly and Ashleigh held her gaze for seconds longer, acknowledging the totally unexpected—and completely foreign—spark between them.

Oh, God...finally a spark. Not from James Simpson, no, but from another girl. Gina Granbury.

Embarrassed, she turned away, walking quickly to a lounge chair and plopping down. She grabbed a towel to cover her face, pretending the need to dry herself. She heard laughter and splashing, knowing the others had jumped in. She lowered the towel, making an effort to keep her eyes from straying to Gina. It didn't matter though. She knew she would go over to talk to her. She had to. It wasn't every day that she got chills just from looking into someone's eyes.

CHAPTER SIX

Present Day

Gina had spent most of the week debating—mainly with herself—whether she should go back to Calloway for the reunion or not. Her decisions ranged from definitely not going to probably not going to *maybe* going. The *maybe* was garnered after Tracy turned into a therapist one evening while they shared a bottle of wine in Gina's tiny apartment above the office.

"Did you ever think the reason you haven't settled down with anyone is because of the way things ended with Ashleigh?"

"That's ridiculous."

"Is it? You broke up with her, then slept with practically everyone in school, me included."

Gina felt her face blush. "Do you have to bring that up?"

"Well, it's the truth."

"You never told Sammy, right?"

"God, no. Husbands don't need to know everything that went on in college." She raised her glass in Gina's direction. "At least it reaffirmed to me that I was straight."

"And it taught me not to sleep with friends."

Tracy laughed. "Which is why you had so few friends back then. You slept with everyone else." She nodded when Gina went to refill her glass. "But back to Ashleigh. You were best friends in high school, you end up having an affair, you go off to college together, then you break up with her. And you've not seen her since."

"So?"

"So in high school, how did you end up being lovers? I mean, from what you've told me, it was a small town where everyone knew each other's business. You surely weren't *out*, were you?"

"Are you kidding? She was a cheerleader."

Tracy frowned. "A cheerleader? Was she sleeping with boys, too?"

"No. Gross. They just believed us when we said we were saving ourselves for marriage." Gina laughed. "Actually, I never dated anyone once I gave Brian the slip. He was the quarterback. He went on to greener—and easier—pastures."

"And Ashleigh?"

"Ashleigh went out with a guy occasionally, James Simpson. He was crazy about her. She broke his heart when she wouldn't be his girlfriend."

"And yet no one suspected you two?"

"No one seemed to think it odd that we spent nearly all our time together. I mean, we were best friends."

"Best friends and lovers?"

"We were inseparable."

"Yet no one knew?" Tracy leaned closer. "So tell me, how did you end up sleeping with a cheerleader?"

CHAPTER SEVEN

Twenty-three years earlier

"You don't talk much, do you?"

Gina wished she had sunglasses to shield her eyes as Ashleigh Pence sat down beside her. The black bikini revealed far more than it hid and Gina's gaze strayed to Ashleigh's breasts before she could stop herself.

"I'm Ashleigh, by the way."

"I know," Gina said stupidly.

Ashleigh arched a perfectly plucked eyebrow, waiting.

"Gina. Gina Granbury."

Ashleigh leaned closer, her eyes holding Gina's captive. "I know," she whispered.

Gina found it hard to breathe as the object of her teenage fantasies sat so close to her. And if Gina had all her wits about her, she'd swear Ashleigh was flirting. Of course, why would Ashleigh Pence—cheerleader—flirt with her?

"So, you don't talk much, do you?" Ashleigh said again.

"No." Gina smiled and tried to relax. The others were splashing in the pool, not paying them any attention. And here they sat, side by side on chaise lounges, bare legs stretched out, soaking up the sun. She chanced another glance at Ashleigh, finding her still watching. Her heart lodged in her throat and she looked away quickly.

"Gina?"

Gina slowly turned, deciding right then and there that she *loved* the way Ashleigh said her name.

"You know Brian thinks you're hot, right?"

Gina rolled her eyes. "If he only had a brain."

Ashleigh laughed out loud, then covered her mouth as the others looked their way. "Not only does he *not* have a brain, he's an asshole."

She glanced to the boy in question and Gina followed her gaze. Sure, Brian was cute. And he was slated to be the starting quarterback on next year's football team, and most of the girls would give their right arm to date him. But he was crass and conceited and so full of himself—even if Gina wasn't totally enamored with Ashleigh, she'd still have no interest in Brian.

"Is that why I got invited?" she asked, the realization dawning on her.

"Jennifer didn't tell you?"

"No." She shrugged. "I thought it was strange for her to invite me."

"Why did you come?" Ashleigh asked.

Gina felt a blush cover her face and she nervously twisted the edge of her towel between her fingers. She shrugged again. "I thought...well, I thought it'd be cool to hang out with you guys." She nearly jumped when she felt a warm hand touch her arm.

"Cool or not, I'm glad you came."

Gina stared at the hand touching her. Her flesh felt like it was burning. Finally, Ashleigh released her and Gina brought her eyes up, colliding with blue ones that held just a hint of a challenge in them.

"And don't take this the wrong way, but I don't think you'll fit in with this crowd."

Gina pulled her eyes away, focusing on the group splashing in the pool. No, she didn't really think she'd fit in with the cool crowd. Not enough to hang out with them. It was just nice getting invited for once.

"I said not to take it wrong." Ashleigh reached for the suntan lotion and poured some into her palm. "They're shallow and they have no goals," she said. "You don't strike me that way."

"Thanks." Gina was mesmerized as she watched Ashleigh spread lotion on her legs.

"School will be out in a couple of weeks. Do you have plans for the summer?"

"Just basketball camp," she said. "I go every year."

"Where?"

"San Antonio."

"Is that why you're so good? Because you go to camp?"

Gina blushed yet again. "I've been playing since I was a kid. My dad loves basketball."

Ashleigh laughed, noticing her blush. "So you're shy and you don't talk much. Yet..."

"Yet?"

"Yet sometimes I'll catch you watching—"

"Come on, girls. Time to get wet!" Brian said as he grabbed both hers and Ashleigh's arms.

Ashleigh managed to pull away from him. "I just put lotion on. But take Gina," she said, smiling as she motioned them away.

Gina must have had a panicked look on her face when she glanced back at Ashleigh. The other girl gave her a reassuring smile and nodded, leaving Gina no choice but to follow Brian to the pool. She pretended to enjoy the banter of the others as she splashed in the water with them, but she was conscious of the blue eyes that watched her, eyes that didn't shy away when she chanced a glance in Ashleigh's direction.

She was totally confused. It was one thing to know she had an enormous crush on the girl, but it was a crush she dealt with from afar, never having to face Ashleigh. Now, because she'd accepted the invitation to the stupid swim party, she'd had to talk to Ashleigh face-to-face. Not only that, Ashleigh had *touched* her. And not only that, but she'd swear Ashleigh was flirting with her. Which meant only one thing—Ashleigh knew of her little crush.

So was she just playing with her? Teasing her? Gina held on to the side of the pool, her eyes sliding across the concrete patio to the chaise lounges, finding Ashleigh watching her again. Their eyes held, the intensity so strong Gina nearly lost her grip on the side of the pool. No, that look wasn't teasing. And *that* confused her even more.

CHAPTER EIGHT

Present Day

Ashleigh stood at the window, her gaze absently traveling over the high-rise offices of the adjacent buildings in downtown Houston. Her office, while not huge, was certainly large enough to compare with some of the executive clients she had. One wall was comprised of nothing but glass, giving her an expansive view of downtown. A view she once craved and even enjoyed.

She turned away from the sight, sitting down in her luxurious leather chair with a heavy sigh. She hated her job. Actually, she hated her life. Twelve years she'd been fighting the daily traffic of this huge city. Fighting it so that she could come here to Peters, Wells, Hancock and Bayer, a prestigious law firm whose clients included the most successful—and powerful—in the oil and gas business. Her specialty was loopholes. She'd written countless contracts with hidden loopholes, most to skirt environmental laws. And she could find even the most inconspicuous loophole written by competing attorneys, saving her clients millions of dollars in the process. She'd argued contracts with juries and judges, convincing them of loopholes, even if there were none. She was good at her job, yet she hated it.

As Pam had said, she had a cushy job with an outrageous salary. It allowed her to live in a very expensive condo surrounded by green in this city of concrete—a hike and bike trail and a golf course, both of which she enjoyed. She was a small-town girl, still not used to the city. She doubted she'd ever embrace the city wholeheartedly, but it was where her profession had taken her. Far from the small south Texas town of Calloway.

She sighed again, spinning around in her chair to face the windows once more. Her class reunion was less than two months away. She'd convinced herself she had no choice but to go. It was expected. It wasn't like she never saw those people. She did. She visited her parents a handful of times each year and she always ran into someone from her class who'd never moved away. They'd been talking about their twentieth reunion for the last two. And really, it was something she'd normally look forward to. Except this year, she had a nagging feeling that *she* would be there. And she wasn't certain she could handle it.

Which was just crazy. She hadn't seen Gina since their first semester of college. In fact, she rarely even gave her a thought. *God, that's a lie.*

She stood up quickly, again going to the window, staring out but seeing nothing. Truth was, Gina Granbury crossed her mind far more than she should. A teenaged affair that ended badly— that's all it was. Yet, nearly twenty years later she still hadn't found anyone who touched her like Gina had. The intensity between them—the heat and the passion—was something she'd tried to duplicate without success. Whether it was a product of teenage hormones or not, the sex between them was...well...simply incredible. And so far in her adult life, nothing had come close.

She spun around, feeling the warm blush on her face. She closed her eyes, letting in images she'd tried to suppress all these years. Images of the two of them, naked and aching for each other's touch, images of stolen moments where they'd hidden

25

in dark shadows, images of hot, wet kisses where they couldn't bear to part. And images of sunshine and high grass, a blanket and a forgotten picnic lunch, their hands and mouths unable to pause even long enough to *pretend* they were on a picnic. No, the precious moments when they were alone were spent doing one of two things—talking or making love.

Her hands balled into fists, squeezing tightly. She chased those images away and replaced them with others that were much more painful. The one of Gina breaking up with her, her tall frame striding purposefully away from her, and then more, images of Gina kissing other girls, Gina laughing with someone else as she teased her, Gina coming out of another girl's dorm room at midnight, her hair and clothes in disarray, evidence of what she'd just done.

Damn her.

CHAPTER NINE

Twenty-three years earlier

Ashleigh closed the door to her bedroom and plopped down on the bed. The sounds of chatter and laughter wafted up the stairs as her brother and sister shouted out names of their friends. Their mother had just given them the okay to each invite one friend along for their week's vacation at the beach. It was a trip they took every summer in June, renting a beach house on Mustang Island. The last two summers, Ashleigh had invited Crissy and her mother assumed Crissy would go again.

Ashleigh stared at the phone on her desk. Crissy would be expecting to go. They were friends. Most thought they were best friends. She rolled over onto her side, tucking her hands against her cheek. Despite what everyone thought, she didn't really have a best friend. She and Crissy never talked about anything other than boys or cheerleading or their group of friends. There was never anything deeper. Their conversations were as shallow as their friendship.

What she really wanted to do was invite Gina Granbury to go with her to the beach. But did she dare? School had been out almost three weeks already and she'd not seen her since the last day at school. She'd caught up to her just before Gina had sped away on her bike. Ashleigh offered to give her a ride home in her car. As they'd stared at each other, Ashleigh realized how stupid her offer was—and transparent. Gina would have to catch another ride back to the school to retrieve her bike. In the few seconds that their eyes held, Ashleigh nearly blurted out that they'd put the damn bike in the back of her car, anything to spend time with Gina. But she was too late. Gina gave her a wink and a slow, knowing smile as she pushed her bike away.

Ashleigh rolled over onto her back again, staring at the ceiling. After the swim party, she'd made it a point to talk to Gina at school. Each time she did, the pull was stronger. It was almost as if she *craved* her nearness. She didn't understand it. Not completely. It was . . . it was an attraction, yes. She swallowed and closed her eyes. There was nothing sexual, of course. She wasn't one of *those* girls.

Was she?

No, of course not. Just because there wasn't a spark with any of the boys in Calloway didn't mean there'd *never* be a spark with a boy.

She eyed the phone again. She really wanted Gina to go. She wanted to get to know her. She had a feeling their friendship wouldn't be shallow. So she stood quickly, pulling out one of the drawers of her desk and finding the Calloway phone directory. There were two Granburys listed. She picked up the phone and dialed the first one, her heart pounding nervously as it rang.

A lady answered with a cheery "hello" and Ashleigh let out her breath.

"May I speak to Gina, please?"

"Oh, dear, I'm sorry. She doesn't live here. This is her Aunt Lou."

"Okay. I'll try the other number."

She hung up quickly, embarrassed. She stared at the second

number, memorizing it, but decided against calling. She scribbled down the address, noting the street wasn't too far from school. No wonder Gina rode her bike. She grabbed her keys and purse and nearly ran out of her bedroom, taking the stairs two at a time. She ignored Mark and Courtney who were now perched in front of the TV. She found her mother in the kitchen making sandwiches for lunch.

"I'm going to run out," she said, dangling her keys for emphasis.

"Where to? It's almost lunchtime."

Ashleigh leaned her hip against the counter next to her mother. "Mom, I don't think I want to invite Crissy to the beach this year," she said.

Her mother glanced at her, then went back to spooning mayo out of the jar. "I thought you had a good time with her last year."

"I did. It's not that. It's just...well, I want to invite a new friend."

"Oh? Who?"

"Gina. Gina Granbury."

Her mother stopped, turning to look at her. "Gina Granbury? I've never heard you mention her before."

Ashleigh shifted her weight, knowing she had no reason to be nervous, yet she was. "She went to Catholic school so she's only been with us since freshmen year. She was at Jennifer's swim party last month," she added, as if that made all the difference.

"I see." Her mother studied her for a moment, then went back to her sandwiches. "Well, honey, you can invite whomever you want."

Ashleigh smiled with relief and leaned closer, kissing her mother quickly on the cheek. "Thanks, Mom. I'm going to run over to her house now, okay?"

"Okay. Be careful."

Ashleigh was nearly giddy as she drove across town. She was too excited to be nervous, and too nervous to even think about what she was going to say to Gina. That is, providing Gina was

29

even home. She may have a summer job. Or worse, she may be at her basketball camp. Ashleigh bit her lower lip. What if her basketball camp was the same week as their vacation?

"Oh, no. Please not that," she whispered to the empty car.

She slowed as she passed the street where she would normally turn for school, going another two blocks before turning left. She drove to the end, watching street signs until she found Gina's. She took a deep breath, turning slowly as her hands tightened on the wheel. Maybe this was too soon. Maybe she should think about it. Maybe she should just call instead.

But as she approached the Granbury's modest house, she found Gina pounding a basketball on the driveway, spinning and executing a perfect jump shot into the torn netting of the basketball rim. She was mesmerized, watching the muscles of Gina's legs as she dribbled, enjoying the fluid grace of her movements, her tan skin, just the barest glimpse of flat stomach as her T-shirt flew up when she jumped again.

Then Gina stopped and turned, their eyes meeting through the windshield of the car. Ashleigh realized she was still in the middle of the street, stopped. She took her foot off the brake, easing into the Granbury's driveway as Gina moved to the side.

Gina bent down and peered through the open window. "What are you doing slummin' on this side of town?"

Ashleigh laughed. "Looking for you."

"Well, you found me."

Gina stepped back, opening the door for her. Ashleigh got out, her nervousness returning as she stood in front of Gina. While not exactly short, Ashleigh still conceded several inches in height to Gina. Gina, too, appeared a bit nervous as she fidgeted with the basketball.

"Is this where you practice?"

"Mostly."

Ashleigh shoved both hands into the pockets of her shorts, trying to appear nonchalant, as if she was used to showing up at a girl's house unannounced. They stood there, eyes darting about—meeting—then quickly looking away, only to come back together again.

"So, are you enjoying the summer?" Ashleigh asked, mentally rolling her eyes at her lame attempt at conversation.

"It's okay. Haven't done anything, really."

"When's your basketball camp?"

"At the end of July."

Ashleigh smiled broadly. "Great."

"Great?"

"Yeah, great." She took a step closer, unable to resist the pull. "You want to go to the beach with me?" she blurted out.

Gina's eyebrows shot up. "The beach?"

Ashleigh nodded. "My family rents a beach house every summer."

"Where?"

"Mustang Island. It's across the bay from Corpus, near Port Aransas."

"Sounds like fun."

"Will you go with me?"

Seconds passed as Gina's eyes searched hers, looking for what, Ashleigh didn't know. She held her gaze, hoping Gina found what she was looking for.

"When...when are you going?" Gina asked, her voice sounding odd to Ashleigh. Gina cleared her throat, then smiled. "I think it'd be fun."

"We go in two weeks. We'll be there over the Fourth and they have a great fireworks show on the beach." Without thinking, her hand found Gina's, and she squeezed her fingers. "Please come." She realized she sounded like she was practically begging and perhaps she was. She couldn't explain it, but she *needed* Gina to go with her.

"Yes." Gina's voice was nearly a whisper. She cleared her throat again. "Of course, I'll have to make sure it's okay with my mother," she said, motioning to the house.

"She can...she can call my mom." Ashleigh went back to her car and found a crumpled piece of paper in her purse. She scribbled out her parents' number, then below that, added the number for her private line. "Here. That's our number. The one on the bottom, that's the number for my bedroom."

"So if I want to talk to your bedroom, I dial that one?"

Ashleigh laughed. "No, silly. You'll talk to me. I'll just be *in* my bedroom."

Again, that invisible pull guided her closer. She couldn't resist it. Gina didn't move away. Ashleigh stood close, trying to think of something to say, something to prolong her visit here.

"Do you...I mean, you and your parents, do you take a vacation during the summer?"

Gina shook her head. "Not really, no. My dad, he works for Ashwood Gas so he's out in the field a lot. If we go somewhere it'll be to see my grandmother over in New Braunfels."

"New Braunfels is fun," Ashleigh said. "They've got that big water park there."

"Yeah. I've been a few times."

"Do you have a brother or a sister?"

"No. Just me. You?"

"Both. They're twins. Ten. They act like they're eight most of the time," she said with a laugh. "And they will each invite a friend to go along too, so be prepared."

Gina nodded and spun the basketball between her hands. "Can I ask you something?"

"Of course. What?"

"Why me?"

Ashleigh felt a blush settle on her face immediately. Yes, why Gina Granbury? Why not someone safer, like Crissy? *Safer?* She tried to think of a reason to give Gina and could come up with nothing other than the truth.

"I want to get to know you," she finally admitted. "I think we could be really good friends."

"You do?"

"Don't you?" Ashleigh held her gaze. "I like you." She wasn't prepared for the fluttering of her heart as Gina returned those words to her.

"I like you, too," Gina said, almost in a whisper.

CHAPTER TEN

Present Day

Gina sped down the highway, the wind whipping at her hair in the open Jeep as she left Corpus Christi behind and headed over the causeway. The island was where she normally went when she needed to think, when a design or a jingle eluded her, or when she just needed some alone time.

Like now.

She turned onto the state park road, flashing her annual pass at the gate. The attendant waved her through without looking. They all knew her Jeep by now. It was a Wednesday in early May and the parking lot at the day-use area was nearly empty. She parked in her usual spot under one of the palm trees and got out, taking a water bottle with her as she walked.

She headed south, her bare feet cooled by the waves as they splashed on shore, then raced back again. Taking a deep breath of the salty, humid air, she let her mind wander where it may as she aimlessly walked, listening to the sounds of the gulls and shorebirds as they came to inspect her, hoping for a handout.

She wasn't surprised to find herself chasing around memory lane again. It was something she'd been doing ever since she got that damn invitation to her twentieth class reunion. She didn't know why it had affected her so. When the invitation for her tenth reunion came, she'd looked at it, shrugged, and tossed it in the trash, not giving it another thought. Of course, ten years ago she was still enjoying the freedom of life in Austin, hanging out with grad students, following the live music scene or relaxing at the lake with a group of rowdy friends. She was content working for someone else, learning her trade at one of the larger advertising agencies in the city, putting in her eight-to-five shift, then forgetting about it until the next morning. She was still in her "whore dog" days, as Tracy called it.

She wasn't quite sure when she finally grew up and realized she wasn't twenty-one any longer. Perhaps it was just one too many hangovers, one too many nameless, faceless women in her bed or one too many unsatisfying affairs.

Or maybe she just got tired of running. Because that's what she'd been doing. Running from her life, running from Ashleigh's ghost, running from a long lost love. Running from her memories.

It was purely by accident that she ran into Tracy, her old friend from college. They'd left San Marcos the day after graduation, Tracy heading home to Corpus and Gina heading to Austin. They'd kept in touch sporadically, finally drifting apart as new friends took their places. She never expected she'd run into her at a grocery store one evening. They'd picked up their friendship where they'd left off, Tracy inviting her for a visit to Corpus to meet her husband and kids. That visit was all it took to convince Gina to leave Austin. The peace she'd been searching for—she found it there, at the beach. The one place that held the most precious memories for her.

She paused, looking out over the gulf, reflecting on the past like she'd been doing for the past couple of weeks. She wondered what Ashleigh's reaction would be if she knew Gina had settled here, having Mustang Island as her playground. They'd come here twice together, once the summer before their junior year of high school, and then again the summer before their senior year. Of course, by the second summer, they were already lovers, sneaking off wherever they could to be together. But it was that first summer that she remembered the most. That summer was one of discovery, of love and longing, of a new friendship that turned into much more by the week's end. Because that was all it took. One short—*one incredible*—week to fall deeply in love with Ashleigh Pence.

CHAPTER ELEVEN

Twenty-three years earlier

"This is our bedroom," Ashleigh said as she placed her suitcase on the dresser.

Gina stood in the doorway, eyeing the one double bed in the corner of the room. *Our* bedroom. *Our* bed. It would be a miracle if she survived the week without making a complete fool of herself. The control she had on her raging hormones was tenuous at best.

"Come on. Let's change."

Gina's eyes widened as Ashleigh pulled her shirt off, standing in nothing but her bra and shorts as she ripped open her bag, searching for her swimsuit. When she found it, her bra joined her shirt on the floor. Gina stood rooted to the spot, her greedy eyes roving over Ashleigh's half-naked body. Being tall and lanky, Gina had no breasts to speak of. In fact, if her mother would allow it, she wouldn't ever wear a bra. But Ashleigh, oh, her breasts were well-formed, standing firm and taut as she slipped on her bikini top.

Gina made herself turn away, knowing she would fall into a dead faint if Ashleigh stripped off her shorts and underwear in the same manner she had her shirt and bra.

"Are you shy?" Ashleigh asked quietly.

Gina didn't turn around as she sorted through her own clothes, trying to decide between the one-piece suit and the bikini she'd dared to include. "I'm a little shy, yes," she said. It was, of course, a lie. She was on the basketball team. She was used to stripping naked and showering in a group stall with ten other girls at once.

"I'm sorry. I'll be more careful."

Gina turned then, finding Ashleigh standing close, her shorts unbuttoned but still on, thankfully. She swallowed, then shook her head, using all her willpower to keep her eyes from straying to Ashleigh's breasts, now covered in the tiny bikini top. "It's okay. I don't mind." She pulled her own T-shirt off, watching Ashleigh's face flush, her eyes darken. She was startled by Ashleigh's reaction. Startled and confused.

Ashleigh's mouth opened and closed several times before words came out. "I...I should...I mean...I could...if you're—"

For the first time in her young life, Gina felt empowered as the truth hit home. Ashleigh was having the same reaction to Gina's body as Gina had had to hers. Without thinking, she pulled her new sports bra off, leaving her as naked as Ashleigh had been earlier. She heard Ashleigh's sharp intake of breath as her eyes settled on Gina's breasts. Gina turned then, her hands shaking as she chose the bikini over the one-piece.

"I'm not that shy," she said, her back still to Ashleigh. "I'm sure by the end of the week, we'll be used to seeing each other."

"I...I guess so," Ashleigh said.

Gina heard the zipper of Ashleigh's shorts and she imagined Ashleigh removing them. She shed her own shorts at the same time, not daring to turn to see if Ashleigh was watching her or not. She slipped on her bikini bottom, thankful she'd spent the last two weeks sunbathing in it. She'd even worn the bikini while she practiced her basketball moves. Her skin was tanned a golden brown, matching Ashleigh's. Most likely, Ashleigh's tan was the result of time spent in the pool, not sunbathing in a lounge chair in the backyard of her parents' house.

When she turned, Ashleigh was watching her, her flip flops held loosely in one hand, a towel in the other.

"You look good," Ashleigh said, her face turning red as the words apparently sunk in. "I mean, that swimsuit looks good on you."

Gina smiled. "Thanks. You look...you look great, too," she said, feeling a blush creep up on her own face. They stared at each other, smiling, finally laughing. And finally relaxing.

"Come on," Ashleigh said, linking an arm with Gina. "Let's hit the beach."

"What do you want to study in college?"

Gina rolled her head to the side, looking at Ashleigh. The other girl was on her stomach, her head resting on her hands. For three days, they'd played in the waves, had participated in a "keep away" game with the four ten-year-olds, had helped them build sandcastles and had played volleyball with a small net Ashleigh's parents had erected. Now, covered in sand and blissfully tired, they lay on beach towels, soaking up the afternoon rays. Ashleigh's mother told them they had two hours until the planned time for grilled burgers, that evening's meal.

"I can't decide," Gina said. "I like to draw, to sketch, but I don't know what I could do with that."

"An architect?" Ashleigh suggested.

"Seeing as how I barely passed geometry, I think not." Gina rolled to her side, facing Ashleigh. "What about you?"

"I still don't have a clue. Business of some sort, I guess. Accounting, maybe." Her eyes slipped closed. "I always imagined I'd have this huge office in a high-rise somewhere. There'd be windows all around and I could see the city, see downtown."

"Moving out of Calloway, are you?"

Ashleigh laughed. "Yes." Her eyes fluttered open again. "I kinda like growing up in a small town, but we're missing so much. Don't you think?"

"Maybe. I like when I go to San Antonio each year. There's so much to do. It's like, no matter what time of day or night, something is always open."

"Yeah. Everything doesn't shut down at five like in Calloway."

"But I like this, too,".Gina said. "I've never been to the beach before. This is fun."

"We've been coming here every year for as long as I can remember."

"You always get to invite someone along?"

"Yes."

"Who came last year?"

Gina watched Ashleigh, seeing the thoughtful expression on her face, the little smile. Gina raised her eyebrows, waiting.

"Crissy. She came the last two years."

"And why not again this year?"

Ashleigh sighed. "I thought we already covered this?"

Gina laughed. "Oh, yeah. You want to get to know me."

Ashleigh flipped onto her side, mimicking Gina. "Why Catholic school?"

"My parents wanted to save me from the corruption of public school," she said with a grin. "It was really my grandmother's doing."

"So you're Catholic then?"

"Technically, I guess."

"What does that mean?"

"It means we don't go to church on a regular basis. Not anymore, anyway. Not since I'm in public school. Back then, they kinda frowned on it when their students didn't show up for Mass on Sundays."

"We're Methodist, technically. Mom and the twins go a lot. Dad never really goes. I used to, but they let me decide now."

"And you don't go?"

"Not as much. I usually leave there with more questions than answers."

"Yeah. I know what you mean."

"It's like, we have a brain, yet we rely on someone else to tell us what to believe, what to think, how to act. I just hate it. Next thing you know, they'll tell us how to vote." She rolled onto her back, staring at the sky. "Maybe I'll be a teacher," she said after a while.

"You'd hate it."

She turned her head to look at Gina. "You think so?"

"No high-rise with a view of downtown."

"Yeah. And I don't think I could deal with kids all day."

They were quiet as they watched each other, and Gina let her eyes roam freely across Ashleigh's face, much as Ashleigh was doing. She finally asked the one question that had been bugging her since the swim party.

"Why don't you have a boyfriend?"

"I don't want one."

"Why?"

"I just...I don't know. None of the guys at school interest me. I don't see the point of having a boyfriend just for the sake of having one."

"But you're a cheerleader. You're one of the most popular girls at school. You're supposed to have a boyfriend."

Ashleigh rolled her eyes. "I hate cheerleading. My mother made me do it when we were in the seventh grade. I've always thought that cheerleaders were nothing but blond, ditzy bimbos," she said with a laugh. "I don't want to be stereotyped that way."

"Well, you have to admit, most are."

"You mean Crissy?"

"She's a little ditzy, yes. But she's in the *in* crowd, just like you."

"I'm only in the *in* crowd because I'm a cheerleader, I live on the north side of town, and my parents gave me a sports car when I turned sixteen. No other reason."

Gina nodded. "The politics of high school."

"Yes. It has its advantages, don't get me wrong," she said. "You get invited to all the cool parties. But I sometimes think I'm growing up too fast. Faster than them, anyway."

"What do you mean?"

"My friends—they're concerned with dating, fashion, celebrities and movies. And gossiping. They're not concerned with their studies, they've not even given a thought to college. They just seem so immature still." She rolled onto her stomach again. "But not you. I think that's one reason I wanted to get to know you better. You're different than them."

"Yeah. I am concerned about college but mainly how I'm going to pay for it. My parents never went to college. My mom, she works part-time at the courthouse. My dad has worked his way up with no college so they're not really pushing me. They said they'd help pay if I went to a junior college, but I don't want that. I want to go to a university." Gina rolled onto her stomach, watching Ashleigh. "That's why I practice basketball so much. If I can get a scholarship, then they'll still be able to help me."

"Wow. My parents have been talking about college for as long as I can remember. I've got a savings account that they started when I was a kid."

"They always told me my college money went to pay for Catholic school."

"Yeah, but that was their choice, not yours. Right?"

Gina shrugged. "I didn't know any better. And it was only recently that I found out my grandmother was the one who paid the tuition, not my parents. I'm just thankful they let me go to public high school."

"Me, too." Ashleigh shifted again, this time to her side, facing Gina. "Did Brian ever ask you out?"

"Yeah."

"And?"

"I told him no." Gina was surprised by the look of relief on Ashleigh's face. "Why?"

"I had heard he was going to. Why did you say no?"

"I'm not interested in him."

Ashleigh smiled. "I don't think anyone's ever turned him down before."

"You?"

"Brian knows I only tolerate him. He would never ask me out." Ashleigh picked up a handful of sand and let it sift slowly through her fingers. "Why don't you have a boyfriend?"

Gina paused, wondering how to answer. "I don't...I don't like them," she finally said. She didn't know if Ashleigh took that to mean she didn't like *boys* or just not the ones in Calloway.

Ashleigh seemed to consider her answer, her eyes peering intently into Gina's, but she didn't probe any further. "Ready to cool off in the water?"

Gina nodded, following Ashleigh into the surf, the water cool on her heated skin. They splashed in the water, jumping waves, then diving headfirst into others, feeling the pull of the tide as they moved into deeper water. When they could no longer touch bottom, they started swimming back to shore, riding the waves in until they stood waist deep. They laughed as a large wave knocked them both down, and Gina instinctively reached for Ashleigh, pulling her back up. It was the first time Gina had touched her, she realized, as her hands slid smoothly across Ashleigh's wet skin, circling her small waist to hold her upright.

They stood there, gazes locked together as the water swirled around them. Gina felt she was drowning in Ashleigh's eyes. They were as blue as the sky on a cool winter's day, holding her effortlessly as Ashleigh peered into her soul, no doubt uncovering the secrets Gina had been trying so hard to keep.

Ashleigh didn't say anything. She simply smiled and squeezed Gina's arm, her fingers lingering, burning her skin.

"Thanks."

Gina couldn't speak. She just nodded. She finally released Ashleigh, her hands falling away from her. Feeling dazed and confused, she stumbled back to shore, snatching up her towel and shaking the sand out of it.

"Gina?"

She closed her eyes, her back to Ashleigh. God, she *loved* the way Ashleigh said her name.

"Are you okay?"

She nodded, feeling Ashleigh move closer. She didn't know what to say. She was afraid Ashleigh knew, afraid Ashleigh could sense the attraction Gina had, afraid Ashleigh would pull away from her.

"It's probably about time for burgers. You ready to head up?"

"Yeah. I'm starving."

Gina winced when her shoulders hit the bed. Her skin was hot. Even the cold shower didn't help.

"Are you as sunburned as I am?" Ashleigh asked.

"Yes. What were we thinking, laying out so long?"

"I don't know but I doubt I'll be able to sleep."

"I feel like my skin is on fire." She lifted up the sleeves of her T-shirt, exposing as much of her shoulders as she could to the cool air.

"We should take our shirts off," Ashleigh said quietly.

Gina froze, the quiet words rattling around in her brain. *Take their shirts off?* Then they would be...*nude.* Her self-restraint was at a breaking point as it was. She'd realized that when they were in the water. How could she possibly stand being in bed with Ashleigh, both of them topless?

She watched as Ashleigh got out of bed, the moonlight bright enough through the thin curtains to follow her movements. She rummaged in her bag, then returned to bed, pausing for only a few seconds before stripping off her T-shirt over her head. Gina felt her breath leave her, felt her heart pound nervously as Ashleigh pulled the covers back.

"Lotion. It might help," she said. She reached over to Gina, tugging at her arm. "Come on. Take your shirt off."

The words were spoken in barely a whisper, yet it was a command Gina couldn't refuse. She stopped thinking, letting her mind go blank, telling herself it was totally innocent. They were both sunburned. They were miserable with their clothes on. The lotion would make them feel better, she reasoned. So she sat up, shedding her T-shirt and tossing it on the floor beside the bed.

43

"I'll do your back," Ashleigh said as she scooted closer.

Gina sat with her legs crossed, her eyes closed, unable to contain the tiny moan that slipped out at the first touch. The lotion did indeed feel cool on her skin as Ashleigh's hands moved softly across the heated flesh of her shoulders. She tried to keep her breathing as normal as possible but she was having a difficult time as those soft hands caressed down her back then up again.

"Turn around."

Again, the whispered command was just that. Gina knew she wouldn't refuse. She turned around on the bed, facing Ashleigh who was kneeling beside her.

"How does it feel?" Ashleigh asked.

"Wonderful," Gina murmured, not caring whether Ashleigh thought she meant the lotion or her touch. She sucked in her breath as Ashleigh touched her collarbone, moving under her neck, her slick hands smooth on her skin.

"You're so soft," Ashleigh whispered. "Yet strong. An athlete."

Gina was finally cognizant enough to notice the shift in Ashleigh's breathing as her hands moved dangerously close to her breasts. The air was thick with tension, the sounds of their breathing, the subtle moans that Gina couldn't contain. She kept her eyes closed, loving the feel of Ashleigh's touch as she moved across her arms, up to her shoulders, around her neck again. Gina's lips parted, her breath coming fast, her heart pounding loudly, so loud she was sure Ashleigh could hear it. Finally, Ashleigh's hands stilled, resting on Gina's forearms.

She opened her eyes, finding Ashleigh's in the shadows. Ashleigh's breathing was as labored as her own and she sat still as Ashleigh's fingers dug into her arms. She finally relaxed, releasing Gina.

"Do you...do you want me to do that to you?" Gina asked quietly, so afraid Ashleigh would say *no*.

"Yes. I want that."

But Ashleigh didn't sit as Gina had done. She lay on her stomach, arms outstretched, exposing her smooth tan back.

Gina poured lotion into her palm, taking a deep breath before touching Ashleigh. She rubbed lightly, both hands moving in unison across her hot skin. She was thrilled by the moan she elicited from Ashleigh. Ashleigh's eyes were closed but her mouth was open as she drew breath.

Gina touched every inch of her back, her fingers memorizing her curves, daring to dip low against her hips, then up her sides, feeling the gentle swell of her breasts as they lay smashed against the bed. Gina had no sexual experience unless you counted the few stolen kisses she'd allowed Carmen last year at basketball camp. But the kissing and touching they'd done felt nothing like what she was experiencing now. If she had any doubts she was a lesbian, they were being answered tonight as her hands moved across Ashleigh Pence's naked flesh.

She sat still, having to clear her throat before speaking. Now it was her turn to command.

"Roll over."

Ashleigh did as she was told, flipping over onto her back. Gina's eyes landed on her breasts, the shadows not enough to hide the erect nipples, the rapid rise and fall of Ashleigh's chest as she breathed. Gina swallowed, her mouth suddenly very dry. She pulled her gaze away, finding Ashleigh watching her closely. She didn't know if she should apologize for staring, but she didn't. She poured more lotion into her hand, meeting Ashleigh's eyes again.

Those eyes closed when Gina touched her and a sensuous moan escaped Ashleigh's lips. Gina's hands moved so slowly, so softly, caressing Ashleigh's skin, no longer even pretending this was about sunburn and lotion. It wasn't. Her breathing was labored now, as was Ashleigh's.

Not knowing whether she was feeling brave and daring—or simply not considering the consequences—Gina let her right hand travel between Ashleigh's breasts to her stomach, her fingers moving in a circular motion. Ashleigh was nearly panting and her eyes fluttered open, finding Gina's. Gina stopped, waiting, afraid she'd overstepped her boundaries, afraid she'd gone too far.

"I love...I love the way you touch me," Ashleigh whispered. She brought her hand up, covering Gina's, pressing it down hard against her side.

Gina waited, not knowing what Ashleigh wanted. Then Ashleigh's eyes slipped closed again and she took Gina's hand, moving it so very slowly up her body. Gina was trembling as she realized Ashleigh's intent. Ashleigh's hand fell back to the bed, leaving Gina's resting just under the swell of her left breast.

Gina hesitated, knowing Ashleigh had left the decision up to her. Gina stared at her breasts, fascinated by the erect nipples, aching to touch them, to feel them against her palm. She didn't pause to think how this would affect their budding friendship, how it would change their relationship. She didn't think of anything except the overwhelming *need* she had to touch Ashleigh.

So she slid her hand higher, not bothering to try to contain her moan as her fingers moved across Ashleigh's breast, the nipple as hard to her touch as she knew it would be. Her hand closed around it, feeling Ashleigh arch higher, hearing Ashleigh's moan as she squeezed her breast before finding the nipple with her fingers, rubbing it lightly, feeling it harden even more.

"*Gina*," Ashleigh breathed. "Please."

Please what? Gina didn't know what Ashleigh was pleading for or what she wanted. Her fingers continued to play with Ashleigh's nipple, loving the sounds that Ashleigh was making. Her whole body was pulsing—*aching*. Then Gina froze as Ashleigh's hand moved between them, moving across her body to graze her fingertips against Gina's breast. Gina sucked in a deep breath as that hand closed over her small breast.

"Oh, *God*," she whispered, her eyes slamming shut.

"You're trembling."

"Yes."

"Do you like the way this feels?" Ashleigh asked, her own fingers now rubbing Gina's nipple lightly.

"*Yes*," Gina hissed, biting down hard on her lip, trying to stop her shaking.

"I want...I want to kiss you. I want us to kiss."

Gina forced her eyes open, her hand still covering Ashleigh's breast, Ashleigh's still covering hers.

"Ashleigh, what are we doing?" she whispered, suddenly afraid. She wanted them to kiss, yes. She wanted them to do all sorts of things. But she was afraid of where it would lead, afraid they would do something that Ashleigh would regret later—tomorrow.

"I'm sorry," Ashleigh said, quickly taking her hand away. "You're right. I'm sorry. That's just crazy."

Right about what, Gina wasn't sure. But she knew one thing. She would get *no* sleep tonight. How could she? She had a throbbing ache between her legs as unfamiliar wetness pooled there. Her body was on fire and it had nothing to do with being sunburned, and everything to do with Ashleigh Pence lying naked beside her.

But she settled back down, next to Ashleigh, their bodies close. The quiet in the room was disturbed only by the sounds of their still rapid breathing.

CHAPTER TWELVE

Present Day

"The fact that you had a female lover when you were a junior in high school is not as shocking to me as learning you were a cheerleader," Julie teased. "That's just wrong. Lesbians should not be cheerleaders."

Ashleigh flicked her gaze to Pam, noting that she was enjoying Julie's teasing as much as Julie was. "Do you have to tell her everything?"

"Of course. You've been our source of entertainment for the last couple of weeks. Why do you think we invited you over for dinner?"

Ashleigh stole an olive off of the snack tray, trying not to take it too personally that Pam and Julie used her for their entertainment. And really, who could blame them. Especially this week, as she had been nearly in a state of panic after the phone call. The phone call from Crissy Summers saying "you'll never believe who RSVP'd." But of course she could. She'd been expecting it—dreading it. She didn't know how she knew, but she would have bet money that this year, Gina Granbury would attend their high school reunion. She could feel it in her gut, feel it in her heart.

And how embarrassing was it going to be to have to face her, seeing Gina, no doubt with a gorgeous lover hanging on her arm, and here Ashleigh would be, forever single. Single and scarred because of Gina, she reminded herself. Single because she couldn't recapture the magic—the passion—that they had. And scarred because Gina Granbury had shattered her heart into tiny pieces, making some lame-ass excuse about them both needing space, needing to see other people, needing to get out. Oh, yeah, Gina got out all right. She got out and into beds, that is.

"Why are you frowning?"

Ashleigh pulled her thoughts back to the present, hating that nearly every waking hour was spent on Gina Granbury, a woman she swore she would hate until her dying breath. She waved her hand dismissively. "Thinking about the breakup," she said.

"The one that was nearly twenty years ago?" Julie asked.

"Look, I know it's hard for you to understand, but I was so in love with her, I thought everything was just perfect. We were truly soul mates. Or at least that's what my perception was at the time. So for her to break up with me barely two months into our college career—well, I was devastated."

"Tell her the story," Pam said as she headed inside. "It's time to put the burgers on."

"You want another beer?" Julie asked, looking at the empty that Ashleigh had been twirling aimlessly on the table.

"Yes, please." *Tell her the story?* What part of the story? The breakup? The falling in love part? Or the part where now, twenty years later, she can still remember what it felt like to be *loved* by Gina Granbury.

"I still can't wrap my head around you being a cheerleader," Julie said as she handed her another beer.

Ashleigh laughed. "I quit my junior year. It was never a passion of mine, only my mother's."

"Is that because you found a new passion?"

"You could say that." She leaned back in the chair, staring out over their backyard. "It's funny, really. Gina knew she was gay. She said she'd known it even before high school. Me? Never crossed my mind. I just knew none of the boys in Calloway interested me, but I didn't wonder why." She paused. "I didn't meet Gina until we were freshmen. I would find her watching me sometimes. We weren't really friends, hardly spoke, but I knew she was there. There was just something about the way she looked at me. I was drawn to her."

"Did she finally get you in a dark corner and kiss you senseless?"

Ashleigh leaned forward, resting her elbows on the table. "Believe it or not, I made the first move."

"I thought you didn't know you were gay."

"I didn't. I invited her on a family vacation that summer before junior year. We always rented a beach house on Mustang Island for a week." She smiled, remembering the excuse for getting naked the first time. "One night, we were both sunburned. We took our shirts off and put lotion on each other. I had no idea her hands on me would feel that good." She swallowed, remembering Gina's hands as they touched her for the first time. "I...I turned it into more. I could tell she was aroused. Hell, we both were. I...I encouraged her to touch my breast. She did. Good God, I thought I was going to pass out." She smiled. "I wanted to kiss her right then, but she pulled back. At the time, I thought it was the best thing to do. The state we were in, it would have gone way past a kiss."

"You didn't freak out?"

"No. I mean, I was a little embarrassed the next morning. She was too. But we didn't talk about it. And we weren't really alone much. My parents had taken us to the mall, then to lunch, then to a movie, so we really didn't have a chance to talk about it." She looked at Julie, smiling. "But that night...oh, *God*."

CHAPTER THIRTEEN

Twenty-three years earlier

"Are you enjoying yourself, Gina?"

"Oh, yes ma'am. It's been wonderful. Thank you for allowing me to come along."

Ashleigh smiled as she eavesdropped on her mother and Gina. She turned the water on, drowning out their conversation as she finished brushing her teeth. When she finished, Gina was leaning in the doorway, waiting. Their eyes met, shyly at first as they both looked away. Then Ashleigh dared to hold her gaze, seeing just a hint of nervousness in Gina's eyes. She assumed Gina saw the same in hers.

They hadn't talked about what had happened last night. They hadn't had a minute alone all day. Even at the movies, her brother Mark wanted to sit by Gina so they were separated. But still, it was different between them. She could tell each time their eyes met, each time they touched, however slight. There was electricity, a spark. And now the twins and their two friends were in bed, her parents were winding down and she and Gina would be off to bed...alone.

"It's all yours," she finally said, motioning to the sink.

"Thanks."

"I'm...I'm just going to go ahead to...to bed," she said, stepping out of the way.

"Be there in a sec."

Ashleigh let her breath out as soon as Gina closed the door. She was nearly embarrassed by her nervousness. What did she think would happen? There were no excuses of sunburn this time so there wouldn't be a repeat of last night.

"Ashleigh?"

She turned, finding her mother watching her. "Yes?"

"Are you okay?"

She felt her face turn scarlet and she stayed in the shadows of the hall, hoping her mother couldn't see. "I'm fine. Why?"

"You've been a little quiet today, that's all."

"Oh, no. Today was fun." She smiled. "I've had a good time this year."

"You're glad you invited Gina?" she asked quietly.

"Yes. Especially since she's never been down here before."

"Well, she's very nice. Mature for her age."

Ashleigh nodded. "Yes. Very different from Crissy, huh?"

Her mother laughed. "Very." She turned away. "Goodnight, honey. Get some rest. Tomorrow will be your last full day on the beach," she reminded her.

"Okay. Goodnight."

She finally escaped into their bedroom, hurrying out of her shorts and into her sleep shirt. She'd just pulled the covers up when Gina came in. She stood at the door, hesitating for a second before she came in and closed it. Ashleigh knew they needed to talk about what had happened, but what would she say? Sorry that I lost my head and groped you? Sorry that I *really* lost my head and wanted to kiss you?

But she said nothing, watching as Gina hit the light switch, plunging the room into darkness. She should have turned her head away, she shouldn't have watched, but her eyes strayed as Gina took her clothes off, then slipped into her own sleep shirt, hiding her small breasts from Ashleigh's gaze. She bit her lower lip, trying to keep her breathing as normal as possible, but Gina wasn't even in bed yet and she felt that pull—making her heart flutter, making her stomach do flips, making her skin tingle.

She wasn't certain how she was going to be able to stand it. For the first time in her young life, she *wanted* someone. She recognized it for what it was. She was sexually attracted to Gina Granbury. She squeezed her eyes shut. Not a boy, no. She never, ever felt this way with a boy. And she knew deep inside she would *never* feel this way with a boy.

"Ashleigh?"

She turned her head slowly, finding Gina standing beside the bed, watching her. "Yes?"

"Do you...do you want me to sleep on the floor?"

"Oh, God...no, Gina. No." She pulled the covers back. "Get in."

Gina got into bed, keeping her distance, which was hard to do in the small double bed.

"I'm sorry about last night," she said. "I shouldn't have—"

"I started it," Ashleigh said, interrupting her apology. She took a deep breath. "Do you want to talk about it?"

"Do you?"

Ashleigh rolled onto her side, facing Gina. "If it were anyone other than you, I'd be totally *mortified* over what happened."

"What do you mean, other than me?"

"Because if it were someone else, it would have just been experimenting, playing around. We would blow it off, go back to school and then worry that the other one would tell someone what happened."

"But?" Gina whispered.

"But it wasn't just experimenting." She met Gina's eyes, the shadows making it hard to read them. "Was it?"

"No," Gina said, the word just a whisper. She cleared her throat. "There's something I should tell you."

53

"Okay."

"Please don't be mad at me. I should have told you sooner."

"Okay," Ashleigh said again.

"I'm...I'm gay."

Ashleigh wasn't sure how to respond. She wasn't shocked, no. But what did she say? *Gee, that explains all that touching and heavy breathing last night.* Of course, she was the one who started it. What did that make her?

"Ashleigh? I'm sorry—"

"No. No, don't. I just don't know what to say," she admitted.

"I promise I won't ever tell anyone what happened. The secret is safe."

Ashleigh smiled. "Oh, so you think it was just one sided?" She reached her hand out, daring to touch her. She found Gina's arm and slid her hand up, rubbing lightly. "Gina, what happened last night...I'm not mad or upset. And the fact that I'm not scares me a little." Just touching her arm now, feeling her warmth, scared her a little. "I wanted you to touch me," she quietly. "We both know I started it."

"Why?"

"Because I'm attracted to you." Saying it out loud made it all the more real. "Last night, I wanted...I wanted your touch. I wanted to kiss you. The way it felt last night...I've never experienced that before. It felt so good," she said.

"Do you...do you want to do it again?"

The question hung in the air, the meaning sinking home. Ashleigh felt her stomach tighten, felt her heart jump into her throat, felt the tightness of her chest as her breathing increased. Did she want to do it again?

"*Yes,*" she whispered.

She waited, wanting Gina to make the first move, wanting her to take the lead. She did, rolling to her side, facing Ashleigh. Ashleigh held her breath, waiting for her touch. She didn't have to wait long before a warm hand slipped under her T-shirt. Tonight, Gina wasn't shy, her hand sliding to Ashleigh's breast without hesitation. Ashleigh gasped at the first touch, then moaned as

54

Gina's fingers teased her nipple.

"Can I take your shirt off?" Gina asked, her voice thick with emotion. "Please?"

"Yes." Ashleigh leaned up, helping Gina pull her T-shirt over her head. "Yours too."

Gina did as she asked, tossing her shirt aside without looking, her eyes locked on Ashleigh. Gina's demeanor was different tonight. Gone was the shyness, the uncertainty. She had a nearly predatory look about her which excited Ashleigh much more than it frightened her.

When Gina's hands came to her again, Ashleigh felt her body rise up to meet her. Her soft moan turned into a groan as Gina covered both her breasts, squeezing them, teasing them, rubbing her hard nipples into her palms. She felt the pulsing between her legs and she squeezed them tightly together. Then Gina pulled her hands away, replacing them with her mouth.

"Oh, dear *God*," Ashleigh murmured, unable to contain the loud moan as Gina's hot mouth sucked at her nipple. Never in her life had she imagined it would feel this way. Her hands reached out, finding Gina, drawing her near. She didn't know what she wanted, didn't know what to do, but she had an innate desire to feel Gina pressed against her.

Instinctively, her legs spread, allowing Gina inside. She was panting now, unable to catch her breath, her hips moving wildly.

"Shhh," Gina whispered, her mouth mere inches away.

Tonight, Ashleigh didn't ask. She just reached up, her hand curling behind Gina's neck, pulling her mouth to her. There wasn't anything shy about their first kiss. Her mouth opened, letting Gina's tongue inside. The few make-out sessions with boys told her that Gina had much more experience in kissing than she did. Gina's tongue captured her own, their moans mingling as their kisses deepened. Ashleigh was completely out of control and totally at Gina's mercy. When Gina stretched out between her legs, when her pelvis pressed down hard against her, Ashleigh was powerless to resist. Her hands cupped Gina's hips, feeling the cool cotton of her panties, the only clothing they both still wore. She pulled Gina hard against her, her moan swallowed by Gina's mouth.

She wanted more. So much more. She didn't care that her parents were only two doors down. She would simply *die* if she didn't have more. She tore her mouth away, struggling to draw breath.

"Touch me," she whispered. "I want you to touch me."

It wasn't a request and Gina—thankfully—didn't take it as one. Her hand slipped inside her panties, Ashleigh too aroused to care about the outcome. She was shocked by how wet she was, shocked by how badly she wanted Gina's touch.

But Gina paused, her fingers dangerously close as she rested her forehead against Ashleigh's, their breathing labored, the sound loud in the small bedroom.

"Ashleigh, are you sure?"

No, she wasn't sure. She wasn't sure of anything. But at this moment, right now, she was *sure* she wanted Gina to touch her. And if she touched her, yes, she knew what would happen. She wasn't that naïve.

Yet she didn't speak. She pulled Gina's mouth to hers, their kisses slower now, lingering, making her want even more. "I'm sure," she finally said, her lips still pressed against Gina's. She was surprised to feel Gina's hand tremble. Gina seemed so in control, so sure of herself.

"Are you a virgin?" Gina whispered.

"Yes." Then, "Are you?"

"Yes." Gina dipped her head again, her lips barely touching Ashleigh's. "I've never done this. I don't have to...to go inside," she said, her tongue wetting Ashleigh's lips. "I can just do this," she said as her fingers finally moved, sliding into the wet crevice between her legs, touching her most sensitive part.

"*God...*Gina," she said, her hips jerking, feeling Gina's fingers as they moved across her swollen flesh. Ashleigh had never had an orgasm. She'd masturbated, trying so hard but it always eluded her. She knew tonight she'd finally know what it felt like as her thighs parted, giving Gina more room. She couldn't believe the intense pleasure she was experiencing. She had nothing to compare it to. She was panting, struggling to breathe, and totally out of control, giving herself completely to Gina, letting her do as she wished—her mouth at her breast, her hand between her legs. Ashleigh felt a pressure build from deep within, growing powerful, pulsing through her. She felt the tightening of her muscles, felt her body contracting. It was exactly like she'd read in romance books—a giant wave, growing stronger, rushing in, threatening to swallow her, then tossing her up, falling endlessly as her body exploded.

She would have screamed, she tried to scream her pleasure, but Gina's mouth was there, stifling the sound, Gina's fingers still resting between her thighs. Ashleigh pulled Gina tight against her, their small breasts smashing together. She was trembling now, uncontrollably, and Gina gathered her close, her mouth moving softly across her cheek, kisses soothing her, hands rubbing, calming.

Ashleigh wasn't certain she could speak, and even then she didn't know what she'd say. At least she wasn't crying. Or worse, freaking out and hysterical. She'd just had her first sexual experience, her first orgasm. And it was with another girl.

She relaxed. Yes, it was with another girl. A girl whose mouth was nibbling at her neck, whose fingers were lightly trailing across her body, whose weight still rested between her thighs. And it felt...*wonderful*.

"I want to touch you that way," she whispered, finally finding her voice. "Do you want that?"

Gina rolled over, taking Ashleigh with her, reversing their positions. Ashleigh found herself on top of Gina, slipping between Gina's thighs as her legs parted. She felt Gina's wetness against her belly, evidence of how aroused she was. It was at that very moment—lying between her legs—that Ashleigh knew she was falling in love. Falling in love with another girl. She was consumed with a need to give pleasure to Gina, a need to touch her, to know *all* of her. The feeling was so powerful, it was frightening.

She met Gina's eyes, the wonder of it all reflected back at

57

her. Ashleigh smiled, then leaned closer, closing the gap between them, their mouths meeting again, soft kisses turning hot. She moved her hand down Gina's body, touching the panties she still wore.

"I want these off," she said. "I want to feel all of you. I want to feel how wet you are."

And she wasn't afraid.

CHAPTER FOURTEEN

Present Day

Gina left the city behind, the sun's first light barely showing in the eastern sky. The morning was cool, the wind already freeing her. She left the top down on the Jeep, needing the openness it brought. She was nervous. So nervous, in fact, she'd nearly cancelled the whole trip. But Aunt Lou was expecting her, and Gina remembered how excited she was at the news Gina would be in Calloway for a week.

She smiled as she turned off the highway past Lake Corpus Christi, taking the back roads through the ranch lands of south Texas. She hadn't heard from any of her classmates in twenty years. Yet, in the past week, she'd talked to Crissy Summers three times as she helped Gina with her hotel reservations, saying even the locals were staying at the Holiday Inn so they could party all weekend. But it was the last conversation that threw her.

"Oh, Gina, it'll be so good to see you. And I spoke with Ashleigh Pence and let her know you were coming. I bet the two of you can't wait to catch up."

Oh, yeah. Can't wait.

Gina wondered if Ashleigh would bring her lover. Hell, would Ashleigh even speak to her? Their breakup didn't go well, and even though Gina did it for Ashleigh, the look in Ashleigh's eyes ...well, it was a look that haunted her for a long time afterward. Every time they would run into each other during the semester, Ashleigh had the same look—wounded and hurt and devastated. It was something Gina never understood. She also never saw Ashleigh with her new lover, so maybe that didn't last after all.

When the semester ended, Gina went to San Antonio where her parents had moved, and she assumed Ashleigh went home to Calloway. Ashleigh didn't return the next semester and Gina spent it trying to forget she and Ashleigh were ever lovers in the first place. Actually, she spent the next several *years* trying to forget Ashleigh Pence. But no matter how many women passed through her bed, no matter how many lovers she had, none of them could ever make her forget Ashleigh...and none were able to replace her.

So she'd settled in Corpus and put all her energy into their business, rarely going out, rarely dating. And seldom sharing her bed with anyone. She was content now, satisfied with her life. Their business was thriving, she had a handful of good friends, especially Pat and Carly. And Tracy and her family filled a void that her parents' divorce had created. Tracy went all out for each and every holiday and Gina was always invited to share it with them. Yes, she was content now.

So why then was she heading to Calloway? So what if it's been twenty years of water under the bridge. She knew seeing Ashleigh would affect her, especially if Ashleigh was there with her lover or her partner or whoever. She was just setting herself up for a deluge of memories.

Yeah, like she hadn't been traveling that road lately. And that was really the problem. She'd been plodding through her memories, reliving those teenage years, still able to remember the tingly feeling she got from being with Ashleigh—touching her, kissing her, loving her. It was the best time of her life, a time when she thought life was perfect, a time when she was so certain that she and Ashleigh would be together forever. A time before the heartbreak and pain. Those were memories she'd just as soon not relive—the breakup and then her cure for Ashleigh—sleeping with any and every girl she could. Anyone to try to make her forget Ashleigh...forget Ashleigh and her new lover.

She was surprised how much that still hurt. Twenty years later she could still feel the sting, still feel the jealously, still see the other girl's face. She smiled, finding some humor. She could remember her face but she couldn't remember her name to save her life.

Ashleigh exited off the interstate east of San Antonio, then turned south, taking the familiar country road to Calloway. She still had nearly an hour's drive but her nervousness increased tenfold as she left the highway. She could have flown from Houston to San Antonio and rented a car, or taken her mother's offer to be picked up, but she wanted this time to think, to prepare.

First of all, she was still shocked that Gina was even going to the reunion. As far as she knew, none of their classmates had ever heard from her in the last twenty years. But nervousness and trepidation had replaced the shock weeks ago, so much so that she'd actually called Crissy to tell her she wasn't going. That plan obviously fell through. Crissy was so excited about the whole affair, Ashleigh just didn't have the heart to cancel.

So now her nervousness was mixed with a healthy dose of anxiety, the feeling of dread weighing heavy on her chest. Which, as she'd been telling herself for the last fifty miles, was ridiculous.

Gina Granbury meant nothing to her anymore. She was a former classmate, that's all. She had no bearing on her life and it was just *crazy* to be dreading her twenty-year reunion because of her.

"So I'm crazy," she murmured. Because, yeah, she *was* dreading it. The only silver lining she could find was that Crissy had said Gina had sent in her RSVP for only one. Which meant Ashleigh wouldn't have to be subjected to seeing Gina with her lover. Well, regardless, she had already decided that if Gina asked if she was seeing someone, she was going to lie and say yes. She'd be damned if she'd let Gina know she was still single.

She tried to imagine how it would go when they saw each other. She didn't want to cause a scene so she couldn't very well ignore Gina. After all, they'd been best friends in high school. None of their classmates ever knew of their affair and as far as she knew, none would know now that Gina was gay. Ashleigh? Yes. After that first semester when she'd returned home for the holidays, she'd been in such a state of shock, still heartbroken, that she'd come out to her parents, had come out to Crissy. She never told them who it was, never mentioned Gina's name. To their credit, her parents hadn't totally freaked out, at least not in front of her. Mark was the one most shocked, but Courtney had put her hands on her hips and smiled. "Cool. My sister's a lesbian. I guess you're not as uptight as I thought you were."

Ashleigh laughed. This coming from a thirteen-year-old who was as uptight as they came. But all of her studying paid off. Courtney went on to medical school, specializing in—of all things—gynecology.

Which Ashleigh found extremely funny, seeing how she was practically celibate, yet her sister made a living touching female bodies.

She tilted her head. What did she mean *practically* celibate? It had been more than a year since she'd slept with anyone. In fact, since she couldn't recall exactly when it was, it may very well be creeping up on two years.

"Yeah, *practically* celibate."

Which brought her back to her original thought. How would her first encounter with Gina go? Would they hug and exchange pleasantries? Would they only shake hands and be cool toward each other? Would they say "hello" and "how are you" and then go their separate ways, never to speak again? Or would someone like Crissy, who had no knowledge of their past, push them together at every chance, thinking they'd have so much to catch up on? Yes, that was the scenario she envisioned. And since she didn't want to cause a scene and draw attention to them—and their past—she would no doubt go along with it.

She sighed, watching the miles speed by as she got ever closer to Calloway. She wondered what Gina was like now, wondered if she'd changed much. The shy girl in high school had come out of her shell as soon as they'd become lovers. She became more outgoing, more sure of herself, confident and strong. Traits that Ashleigh loved in her. Of course, after their breakup, Gina continued to be outgoing, sleeping with nearly every girl at college, whether they were single or not. Or gay or not, Ashleigh recalled, as she remembered a handful of straight girls falling victim to Gina's charm.

Damn her.

Gina was shocked by how much Calloway had changed. Aunt Lou had told her that their sleepy little town was growing as more and more people escaped the city, leaving San Antonio and moving south, but she never imagined this. The tiny two-lane road that she remembered was now a highway, bypassing the heart of town as it looped around to the north, no doubt built for commuters who still drove into the city to work every day.

She took the business route into town, now looking somewhat familiar as many of the old buildings remained, housing locally owned shops that were still in business. Even the movie rental and tanning place was still there, although back then, it was called The Corner Tan. She was surprised that a Blockbuster hadn't opened in town, putting it out of the movie business.

She drove on, wanting to stop by Aunt Lou's before checking in at the hotel, as she had a couple of hours before the planned happy hour "get reacquainted party." She and her aunt had always had a special bond, but it wasn't until she was older that she realized why. Aunt Lou was a lesbian. It was something they had never talked about. Ever. Oh, they talked about Gina and her love life plenty. But any time Gina questioned Aunt Lou's lack of a husband, a partner, she'd clam up, saying she was perfectly happy being an old maid. Of course, Gina eventually put two and two together, remembering Aunt Lou's trips to San Antonio and even the occasional "friend" she'd have over. Gina had been too young to question it, to think it odd. But now, as an adult, she knew that Aunt Lou had had a lover in San Antonio. Whether she still did, Gina had no clue. She respected Aunt Lou's need for privacy, for secrecy, and left it at that. If she ever wanted to confide in her, she would. If not, it wasn't any of Gina's business. She suspected one reason Aunt Lou remained deep in the closet was she didn't want Gina's mother to use her as the excuse for Gina being gay. Her mother *still* found it difficult to accept and still felt the need to let her know how disappointed she was.

Gina shook her head, not wanting to go there. She and her mother's relationship had been strained, to say the least. First their divorce, then Gina coming out to them, then her father's sudden death and then her mother remarrying—all events which widened the gap between mother and daughter. Oh, they weren't estranged or anything. They still talked on the phone occasionally, they were civil, but they didn't see each other. Gina rarely left the coast, content with the extended family she'd built there. Her mother had come once to visit, to see where Gina worked and lived, but the disapproval Gina saw in her eyes, not just about her lifestyle, but about her life in general, was enough to keep Gina from extending the invitation again. She knew Aunt Lou and her mother still kept in touch, so she wondered if her aunt had felt the need to share that Gina was coming to stay the week with her.

She turned down the familiar street, the homes all older and showing their age, but her aunt's yard was as pristine and well-kept as Gina remembered. She parked and got out of her Jeep, stretching her legs and back after the long drive. She ran her fingers through her hair, windblown and disheveled as it was. She tried to tame the dark strands, finally giving up.

"Oh, my God, look at you."

She turned, finding Aunt Lou rushing toward her. She

opened her arms, accepting the tight hug and kiss on her cheek. She pulled back, grinning.

"Good to see you, too."

"You look wonderful, Gina. As lovely as ever. Your father would have been so proud of you," she said as she grasped her shoulders.

"Would he?"

"Gina, of course he would," she said in that *let's don't talk about it* tone. "Now come inside. Let's catch up."

Ashleigh pulled into her parents' driveway, feeling the familiar peacefulness that always eluded her in the city. Even after the stressful drive and the impending reunion that she now dreaded, the peacefulness returned. She got out, taking a deep breath of the clean, country air, enjoying the quiet for a second before heading up the walk. Her mother was waiting, opening the door before Ashleigh could knock.

"Hi, honey," she said as she pulled Ashleigh into a hug. "So good to see you again."

"Hi, Mom." Ashleigh stood still, knowing she wouldn't be released until her mother was good and ready. She finally loosened her grip and Ashleigh stepped away, grinning. "Good to be home."

"I keep telling you to visit more often," she said, pulling Ashleigh inside. "We'll get your things later."

"Oh, I'm not staying here."

Her mother spun around. "What?"

"Well, not for the weekend. I've got a room at the hotel. Crissy insisted," she said.

"But next week?"

"Yes, I'll stay here."

"Because Courtney would be terribly disappointed if—"

"Mom, I said I'm staying here. It's just the reunion and all, it would just be easier to stay there. I'll come here on Sunday."

"And you'll stay until Wednesday?" her mother asked as she led them into the kitchen.

"Yes. Is Courtney still coming Monday as planned?" She eyed the pitcher on the cabinet. It wasn't tea. She raised her eyebrows.

"She's leaving the hospital Monday morning." Her mother followed her gaze. "It's Friday. Your father expects cocktails when he gets home."

Ashleigh glanced at the clock, then back at her mother.

"I thought you and I might have a drink on the patio. And no, I've not turned into a lush. Your father gets home at four on Fridays."

Ashleigh grinned. "So then Courtney and I don't have to have a daughter intervention?" She watched as her mother filled two glasses of what she assumed were margaritas. "How's Mark?"

"Oh, busy as ever. I just talked to him last week. He said he's missed you the last couple of times you've called."

"Yeah. And apparently he doesn't know how to return calls." She took the drink with a nod. "Thanks."

"He's seeing someone, you know."

"No, I didn't know. Since when?"

"For about a month," she said. "Let's go out to the patio."

Ashleigh stepped outside, the view bringing back a rush of memories. Their backyard was as impeccably neat and tidy as always, the green grass cut to perfection, the water in the pool crystal clear. She wasn't surprised by the direction of her thoughts as she could picture Gina splashing in the pool, laughing at her, playing with her. She mentally shook those thoughts away, turning to find her mother watching her.

"It's beautiful back here," she said, joining her mother at the small round table, the ceiling fan stirring the air around them. "I miss having a yard," she said.

"You can afford a house. Why must you stay in that condo?"

"Because it's a prime location, and I have access to a hike and bike trail, not to mention the golf club." She sipped from her drink. "Besides, if I want to sell, it wouldn't last a day on the market."

"It's still hard to picture you in the big city. I just wish—"

"I'm not moving back to Calloway," she said with a laugh.

"No, but what about San Antonio? Courtney is there and you'd be close to home," she said wistfully.

Ashleigh reached across the table and squeezed her mother's hand. It was a conversation they had nearly every time she visited. "So, tell me about Mark."

"What's to tell? You know how secretive your brother is."

"Okay, let me rephrase. Is he seeing a he or a she?"

"She."

Ashleigh sighed. "So he's still convinced he's bisexual?"

"You would know better than me. I'm just glad he's not seeing that artist fellow any longer."

Ashleigh laughed. "Mother, *Mark* is an artist."

"Exactly. At least one of them needs a real job."

Ashleigh hid her smile. She knew all too well that Mark was still in love with "the artist fellow" and only pretended to date women so that their parents wouldn't feel totally guilty over having two gay children. When Adam ended things with Mark, it'd taken him awhile to recover. She and her brother talked nearly nightly during that time, the closest they'd ever been. But living in San Francisco, he got back in the saddle quickly and their nightly talks ended.

"So, are you looking forward to the reunion?"

Ashleigh spun her glass, watching the ice bounce off the sides. "Yes, it'll be fun," she said, hoping her voice had the correct amount of enthusiasm.

"Well, I spoke with Lou Granbury at the grocery store the other day. She says that Gina will attend this year. Have you talked to her?"

Ashleigh shook her head. "No, but Crissy said she was planning on coming."

"I'm sure that's exciting. I still can't believe the two of you lost touch like that. You were so close during high school."

If you only knew. But Ashleigh forced a smile. "It'll be...good to see her, yes," she said. "I don't think anyone from school has had contact with her over the years."

"She lives down at the coast, Lou says. Corpus."

"Really?" Ashleigh stood, not wanting to continue the conversation. "These were good. Can we have another?"

"Of course, honey. But don't overdo it. You have a big night tonight," she reminded her.

Ashleigh gave her a fake smile, then disappeared into the kitchen for a refill. She would need much more than a couple of margaritas to get her through the night.

CHAPTER FIFTEEN

Present Day

Ashleigh was a bundle of nerves as she pulled into the parking lot of the brand-new Holiday Inn out on the north side of town. She sat in her car, looking about nervously, knowing with her luck, Gina would be pulling in at the same time. But all was quiet as she got out. She took her bag, hurrying across the parking lot to the lobby. She was immediately engulfed in a hug as Crissy ran to meet her.

"Oh, my God," she shrieked dramatically, as if they never saw each other. "I can't believe you're finally here."

Ashleigh returned the hug. "Hi, Crissy. Missed me or just needing moral support?" She glanced around. "Who all's here?"

"Quite a few already. Too many to name. And yes, you were the class president. You should be doing this job."

"But you live here. We agreed *you* were better suited for this job," Ashleigh reminded her.

"Well, it's been a little fun. I'm so glad so many could come up early tonight." She shoved her toward the desk. "Go check in. I'll meet you in the bar."

"Okay." She took a deep breath. "Is Gina Granbury here yet?"

Crissy smiled. "Oh, my goodness, yes. You will not *believe* how she looks."

Ashleigh frowned. What? Did she gain two hundred pounds? Did she shave her head? Was she covered in tattoos? Piercings? What? But before she could ask, Crissy had hurried off to greet a new couple who walked in. The man looked somewhat familiar but Ashleigh couldn't place him. She didn't dwell on him as she turned to the desk, smiling at the clerk as she gave her name.

So Gina was already here. Wonderful. Might as well get it over with. She signed without looking, took the key card without thinking and robotically walked to the elevators, finally glancing at her receipt, finding her room number.

"I should have had one more margarita," she murmured as the elevator whisked her to the third—and top—floor.

She methodically unpacked her bag, walking aimlessly around the room, stalling as long as possible. The happy hour gathering was casual, but what did that mean? Khaki causal? Or summer shorts casual? She eyed the clothes she'd packed, deciding it was Calloway...summer shorts casual would be fine.

So she stripped, taking a somewhat leisurely shower, finally feeling the effects of the tequila as her mood turned from nervous to mellow. And mellow was what she needed if she was to see Gina for the first time in twenty years.

As she dressed, she wondered what her reaction would be. For that matter, what about Gina? Was she feeling any of the trepidation Ashleigh had been fighting for the last month? And what in the world did Crissy mean about how she looked?

Just go down there.

She took a deep breath, staring at herself in the mirror, pleased with what she saw. Her years of activity, of biking and the cursed jogging that Pam insisted on, had kept her in good shape. Her body was toned, her skin tanned, her face clear. She looked *good*. Great, in fact. She ran her fingers through her hair, the layers making her look carefree and...tousled. She blew out a breath, stirring the bangs on her forehead. *Tousled?* Well, she couldn't put it off any longer.

She shoved cash in one pocket and her key card in another, then strode to the elevators, knowing the time had come. She ignored her nervousness, pushing it down, trying to muster up even a little excitement for the evening. She would see old friends, most of whom she'd not spoken to since the tenth reunion. She would renew friendships, she would visit with Crissy, the one person she saw most often, and she would avoid Gina Granbury at every turn.

As soon as she hit the lobby, she heard laughter and loud conversations coming from the bar. The party appeared to be in full swing. She hesitated only briefly before going inside, thankful for the sparse lighting as she stood in the back, her eyes darting around the room. It didn't take long. Like a magnet, she found Gina. She was sitting at the bar chatting with Crissy and another woman whose name eluded her. It didn't matter. Her eyes were locked on Gina.

And as if on cue, Gina slowly turned, sensing—as she always used to do—Ashleigh's gaze on her. Ashleigh waited, her thundering heartbeat deafening in her ears, her pulse pounding, her palms sweating. Now she knew what Crissy meant when she said she wouldn't believe how Gina looked.

Stunning.

Tall and slender, wearing loose-fitting shorts and stylish Teva sandals, her dark hair shorter than Ashleigh remembered, her skin tanned a lovely brown, her face as fresh and appealing as it had been twenty years ago. And the eyes...those dark, expressive eyes...they captured Ashleigh's, holding her, pulling her as they always had.

But she stood rooted to the spot, the others in the room fading as they stared at each other. It was only then that she recognized the nervousness—the uncertainty—in Gina's eyes. Then sounds penetrated, movements blocked her vision, and she saw Crissy

71

wave at her, beckoning her over.

She tried to appear relaxed—cool and indifferent—even though she was as nervous as she could ever remember being. But the awkwardness she felt was short-lived as Crissy tugged on her arm, pulling her face-to-face with Gina Granbury.

"Oh, my God. I can't believe you two haven't seen each other in twenty years," she shrieked. "Hug or something," she said, shoving them together.

It was surreal what happened next. Gina's arms slipped around her, pulling her close and Ashleigh went with it, sinking into the hug, her body coming alive at the contact. It lasted mere seconds, but it was long enough for her to realize her body recognized Gina's, if only on a subliminal level.

"How are you?"

The words were quiet, nearly whispered in her ear. She pulled away, forcing a smile to her face. "Good. Great." Then, "It's been awhile," she said.

Gina didn't say anything, merely nodding. "Want something to drink?"

"Oh, yeah. Definitely." *Definitely.*

Gina raised an eyebrow, an expression Ashleigh used to find extremely sexy. She ignored the lure of the eyebrow and turned to Crissy. "What's everyone having?"

"Open bar, sweetie. Get what you want." She pulled Gina to her feet. "I'm going to steal Gina for a second."

"Sure."

Ashleigh leaned on the bar, impatiently tapping the wooden surface. "Bourbon and Coke," she said. "A double."

"You have a preference?"

"The good stuff," she said, spinning around, watching as Crissy settled Gina at a table. What in the world did they have to talk about?

"Gina, you look absolutely gorgeous. Wait until you see some of the others. Let's just say, time has not been kind."

Gina laughed. "Well, you held up pretty good."

"Darling, a personal trainer and a little Botox does wonders."
Crissy pulled her chair closer. "I want to fill you in on all the
gossip before things get started."

"Okay."

"First of all, and you'll probably be shocked at this, but
Ashleigh Pence is...gay," she said, the last word barely a whisper.

Gina feigned shock. "You're kidding?"

"No, I'm not. Can you believe it?"

"When did this happen?"

"College. She came home after the first semester, heartbroken
and in tears. She confessed she'd had an affair with another girl,
and the girl broke her heart."

Gina leaned back in her chair, surprised that Ashleigh had
gotten that attached to her new girlfriend that quickly. "Well, I'll
be," she said.

"Oh, yeah. It was quite the talk back then. Of course, now,
well, everyone is used to it. I'm surprised you didn't know. I
mean, you two were inseparable."

Gina shrugged. "I guess you don't tell best friends
everything."

"And you remember Robin Weathers?"

"She was a cheerleader, right?"

"Right. Guess what? She joined a convent."

"A nun?"

"Yeah. And she's coming too. That should be interesting.
Ashleigh has turned into a potty mouth. I hope she doesn't let
one of her four-letter words fly around Robin." Crissy stood,
smiling and waving toward the door. "New arrivals. Go mingle.
I just wanted to share the gossip about Ashleigh so you wouldn't
be totally blown away if she told you."

She hurried off, leaving Gina sitting alone. Inevitably her
eyes were drawn back to Ashleigh at the bar. She wasn't sure
what she expected her to look like. In her mind's eye, Ashleigh
was still nineteen, as she'd been the last time Gina saw her. But
the beautiful girl she remembered had grown into a gorgeous
woman, moving with a grace that she'd always possessed. And the

hug? God, how unexpected was that? And awkward. At least for her and no doubt for Ashleigh too.

As she stared, Ashleigh slowly turned. Gina waited, wondering if that old magic was still there. They'd always had a knack for knowing when the other was watching, knowing exactly where the other was in a crowded room. And now, just as Gina had felt Ashleigh's presence earlier, Ashleigh apparently felt Gina's eyes on her. Gina didn't look away when Ashleigh found her. Despite her earlier apprehension over seeing Ashleigh again, the initial shock was over. After twenty years, she thought the least they could do was have a normal conversation.

Perhaps Ashleigh thought the same as she made her way over to the table. Gina was unable to keep her gaze from straying, Ashleigh's shorts showing off tan, muscular legs.

She blushed slightly when she finally raised her head, surprised at the amused expression Ashleigh sported.

"I couldn't for the life of me figure out what Crissy needed to talk to you about. Then it dawned on me."

"You're gay," Gina said with a smile. "And I'm just totally shocked."

"I'm sure you are."

Gina motioned to a chair, silently asking Ashleigh to sit. "And so they think I'm straight?"

"No one has seen you since then. Why would they think otherwise?"

"I just assumed you would have—"

"Outed you?" Ashleigh shook her head. "No. I didn't want to go into all that with anyone."

Gina leaned forward. "So, how have you been?"

"Good. Wonderful, in fact. I live in Houston. I work for a law firm."

Gina raised an eyebrow.

"Yes, I am."

"You're kidding. *You?*"

"Why is it so hard to imagine that I'm an attorney?"

"It's just not what I would have thought." She paused. "Did

you ever get that huge office in a downtown high-rise?"

"As a matter of fact, I did."

"Good for you." Gina brushed the drop of water away that slid down her glass, finally asking the question that had her most curious. "So, are you seeing someone?"

There was only a slight hesitation as Ashleigh glanced at her. "Yes, yes I am. A...a lovely woman. We've been together for a few years now," she said.

"That's great. I'm glad you found someone."

"Yes. It's a...it's Faith," she said. "Her name. And what about you?"

Gina shook her head. "No. Single."

"Really? Still playing the field?"

"What does that mean?"

"Well, the last time I saw you, you were sleeping with practically every girl at school, both gay and straight."

Gina looked away, embarrassed. "Yeah, well, I had a lot of running to do."

"Running from your guilt, perhaps?"

"*My* guilt? What did I have to feel guilty about?"

"Oh, please."

"What? You speak from experience?"

"*Me*? I certainly had nothing to feel guilty about."

"No, you didn't. Why should you? We were kids. I don't blame you."

"What are you talking about?"

"Ashleigh, that's twenty years of water under the bridge," she said, repeating Tracy's words to her. "We don't need to rehash it. I don't expect an explanation or anything." Gina was surprised by the angry flash in Ashleigh's eyes.

"What the *hell* are you talking about?"

Gina shrugged, not certain she wanted Ashleigh to know just how hurt she'd been. Like she'd said, they were kids. Did she honestly expect them to be together forever? Well, yeah, at the time she did. So, she tried again to explain.

"You know, I tried to be the one to take the high road, to

75

let you off the hook," she said. "But let me tell you, the pain I felt that day, it still smarts," she admitted. "If I had to do it over again, I'd make you come to me. I'd make you be the one to end things."

Ashleigh stood up quickly, shoving her chair back. "I don't know what the hell you're talking about, but if you're trying to turn this around and make *me* the bad guy, to somehow blame me for what happened, well...you're goddamn crazy as hell," she said before storming off.

Gina watched her leave, expecting her to exit the bar altogether, but Crissy intercepted her, dragging her off to talk to another couple who had just come in. She reminded herself that Ashleigh had been the class president, had been voted most popular...she'd be expected to talk to everyone, to know everyone. To *remember* everyone. But Gina recognized the squared shoulders, the straight back. She grinned. Oh, yeah, Ashleigh was pissed. She raised her glass in a silent salute. The civil conversation she'd envisioned had soon turned offensive, surprising her a bit. Twenty years under the bridge, sure, but they still had a passion between.

Shame it now involved anger instead of love.

Ashleigh finally escaped from Crissy, heading to the bar for another drink. She knew Gina still sat at the table...alone. And damn if she didn't feel sorry for her. It reminded her of high school, with Gina on the outside looking in. That is, until they... well, until they became friends. And lovers.

"You're the double bourbon? The good stuff?" He wiped the bar in front of her, smiling in that flirty way Ashleigh couldn't stand. "Want another?"

Of course, flirting back meant you *really* got the good stuff. "Twentieth class reunion. What do you think?" she asked with a wink. "Do I need another?"

"Or two." He leaned closer. "And I'd say judging by this crowd, I better keep the bottle hidden for you."

Instead of trying to come up with a witty reply, she dropped

76

a twenty on the bar, hoping the tip would suffice. He slid a fresh drink her way. "You're a good man. Wish me luck," she murmured as she turned away from him, fresh drink in her hand.

Oh, and damn if her gaze didn't bring her back to Gina. But this time, no, she refused to go to her. And really, what was with the garbage Gina was spewing about feeling guilty? Ashleigh knew she had no reason whatsoever to feel guilty about anything. Hell, Gina was the one who—out of the blue—had decided they needed to expand, needed to see others, needed to branch out.

"Fucking bullshit," she murmured.

"Excuse me?"

Ashleigh turned, smiling at...Sherry? No, but damn, what was her name? Janie? She frowned, knowing it was on the tip of her tongue.

"I'm Debra. I wouldn't expect you to remember me. I—"

"We had chemistry together," Ashleigh said, hoping her memory was correct. At the other woman's bright smile, she knew her guess was right.

"You *do* remember. Yes. Mr. Arnold's class. I missed our tenth so I thought I'd make this one."

"Glad you did. There's a good crowd this year." Ashleigh sighed, not wanting to be rude, but not wanting to make small talk with a woman she didn't know. Of course, right then, her alternative was Gina, who was making her way over to the bar.

"Oh, that's Gina Granbury, isn't it?"

Ashleigh nodded. "Yes."

"You two were best friends, weren't you?"

"Yes, we were." Ashleigh looked around, trying to find an escape route. She wasn't certain she could be civil to Gina right now.

"Wow. She's..."

Ashleigh turned to her. "She's what?"

"Gorgeous. I mean, wow. Look around. Most of us look old and married. But she—"

"Excuse me?"

"Sorry. I didn't necessarily mean you." Debra smiled. "Are you married?"

"No."

"Divorced?"

"No."

"Oh?" Then she frowned. "I hope you're not one of those who forsake marriage and just live together. God created marriage for a reason. It's the glue that keeps our traditional families together. Why if it wasn't for marriage—"

Ashleigh held up her hand, stopping her. "Debra, I'm gay. I'm not really interested in your family values speech." Okay, so she would be rude. "I think that's *way* overrated. It's bullshit."

Debra's eyes were wide as she took a step back. "You're... you're gay?"

Ashleigh nodded. "Yes. Very."

Debra took another step back, then glanced at Gina who finally made her way over. Debra looked between the two of them, then took another step back. "I...I need to go."

"Sure. Nice to see you again."

Debra fled and Ashleigh turned to Gina. "Debra something or other." She waved her hand dismissively. "I just told her I was gay."

"Oh. That explains the look of terror on her face." Gina smiled. "Or did you make a pass at her?"

"As if. She was launching into a speech on the benefits of traditional marriage and about to go into the whole family values thing. I was about to vomit." Then she spun around. "And what the hell are you doing over here? I don't want to talk to you right now."

"We haven't seen each other in twenty years. Do we have to fight?"

"Why not? I do believe that's how we ended things twenty years ago. With a fight."

"Do you really want to talk about that again?" Gina leaned against the bar. "Look, I was terrified of coming here. I was actually afraid to see you."

"You were?" Ashleigh relaxed a little. "I was too," she confessed.

"But now that I've seen you, it's not so bad. We're adults now. And that was a long time ago." She shrugged. "Despite the history between us, we were really good friends at one time."

"So you want to forget the history, and just—"

"I just would like to visit and catch up...and not fight. We've both moved on. You more than me since you've got a partner."

Ashleigh was about to protest then remembered her lie. God, *Faith*? Couldn't she have come up with a better name than that? Of course, it was fitting, wasn't it?

"Why aren't you with someone?"

"I just...well, I haven't met the right one yet." Gina downed the rest of her drink. "I know it sounds trivial, but it's the truth. I've not met anyone I want to spend my life with. I may not ever meet her."

"And after all that dating you did?"

"I wouldn't really call it dating, Ashleigh." She turned back to the bar and held up her empty glass, nodding at the bartender. "I finally grew up. I got tired of living that way."

"My mother says you're down at the coast," she said. Gina raised her eyebrows questioningly. "She ran into your Aunt Lou," she explained.

"Oh."

"How long have you been there?"

"About seven years. And you'll probably laugh but, well, I found an inner peace there. I went to visit Tracy, an old friend from college. I ran into her in Austin unexpectedly."

"Was she one of the ones—"

"She's married, got a couple of kids," Gina said, interrupting her question. "It was there that I realized how empty my life really was." She handed over a folded bill to the bartender. "Thanks." She took a sip, nodding. "Anyway, being down there brought back a bunch of memories, as you can imagine."

"Our first time," Ashleigh said quietly, feeling a rush as memories—still fresh—surfaced.

"Yeah. Our first time." Gina leaned closer and Ashleigh didn't shy away from her nearness. "It's something that I'll always hold dear to me. It was special."

"Yes. Yes it was." And for all the bad blood between them, the betrayal, the breakup, it was special.

"You probably are sorry it was me, though," Gina said. "I mean, your first time and all. I'm sure you've met someone that you wish you'd waited for."

Ashleigh shook her head. "At first, after you ended our relationship, yes, I did wish I'd waited." She chanced a quick glance into those dark eyes. "Because I hated you so much. But later, after I'd been...well, when I finally was able to allow someone else close, I realized that what we shared at that young age, well, it *was* special. I wouldn't have wanted it to be anyone other than you."

They both leaned on the bar, quiet. Ashleigh couldn't believe the vein their conversation had taken. After months of dreading the encounter, after weeks of dredging up old memories, here they were, talking about their past as if it conjured up no recollection of pain and heartache. It did. Twenty years later, she could still remember the agony she felt when Gina walked out of her life. It was a heartbreak she was certain she'd never recover from.

Yet, here they were. There'd been no screaming and crying, no angry words. She smiled. Well, the little spat over feeling guilty hardly counted. It wasn't like she'd slapped Gina or anything.

"Why are you smiling?"

Ashleigh turned to face her, their arms brushing. "Because here we are, having a normal conversation, discussing something that was so painful for me, discussing it in a rational manner."

"And that makes you smile?"

"I was thinking about our earlier conversation." She laughed quietly. "Where—in the movies—I probably would have slapped you, causing a scene."

"I see." Gina leaned forward. "It was painful for me, too, Ashleigh. More so, I think."

"More? How could it possibly?"

"You had someone to go to. I didn't."

Ashleigh stepped back. "What are you talking about?

Who?"

"The girl you were seeing. I don't remember her name."

Ashleigh's eyes narrowed. "Gina, seriously, what the hell—"

"There you two are," Crissy said, coming to stand between them, putting an arm on each of their shoulders. "Just like old times, you two huddled off somewhere together. Catching up, are we?"

"Catching up, yes," Ashleigh said. She looked at Gina but she'd turned, facing Crissy.

"I can't get over how wonderful you look," Crissy said to Gina. "I bet you're a knockout in a swimsuit."

Ashleigh couldn't help but smile as Gina's face turned red with embarrassment.

"I did bring a swimsuit, as instructed," Gina said. "However, I'm having a hard time picturing this crowd sitting around the pool, having a swim party."

"Oh, it'll be fun. Brian is in charge of the hot dogs. And like high school, we'll have to sneak in beer. The hotel has a no-alcohol policy out there."

"Brian?"

"My husband," Crissy said.

"Not *the* Brian?"

Ashleigh laughed. "The same."

"Oh, my God. You married Brian?"

Crissy put her hands on her hips, staring at Gina. "I was the head cheerleader, he the star quarterback. It's a fairytale, don't you think?"

Ashleigh could tell Gina was at a loss. The Brian she remembered was a conceited ass. "They've only been married a couple of years," Ashleigh explained.

"Everyone needs time to grow up," Crissy said. "Second marriages. I highly recommend them." She took Gina's hand. "You're still single, right?"

"Right."

"You remember James Simpson?" She pulled Gina with her. "He never married either. Let's go visit."

81

Ashleigh laughed at the panic-stricken look on Gina's face as Crissy slipped into her matchmaker mode. She'd seen James a handful of times over the years. She suspected he was gay—and not out—but Crissy insisted he never married because he was still in love with Ashleigh.

Oh, that was a trying time, she recalled. She and Gina sneaking off whenever they could, just to be together. And James, turning into nearly a stalker as his infatuation with Ashleigh became nearly unbearable. She made the mistake of going out with him once. Her mother insisted. "He's such a nice boy." Yeah, a nice *horny* boy.

CHAPTER SIXTEEN

Twenty-two years earlier

"I don't want to go out with him," Ashleigh insisted.

"He's a nice boy, honey." Her mother clasped both her shoulders, making Ashleigh look at her. "I just don't understand you, Ashleigh. You're a beautiful girl, so popular in school, yet you spend all of your time with Gina. This is when you should be dating, having fun, going to parties."

"I do have fun, Mom." She'd always been able to tell her mother anything, but this...her affair with Gina...no, she was too afraid. "I thought you liked Gina."

"I do, honey."

"Mom, Gina and I...well, she's not like the others. She's interested in college. We talk about our future, about what we want. The others—Crissy—it's all boys and parties and gossip."

"That's how it's supposed to be when you're a teenager," her mother said with a laugh. "I always told your father you grew up too quickly. That's one reason I pushed you into cheerleading."

Ashleigh rolled her eyes. "I hate cheerleading."

Her mother studied her for a moment. "Ashleigh, do this for me? Just go out with him. Give it a chance."

"But—"

"You're going to be a senior. It'll be prom time. Wouldn't it be nice to have a boyfriend?"

Ashleigh bit her lip to keep from laughing. A *boyfriend*.

But she finally agreed, just to get her mother to shut up about it already. She called Crissy, saying she'd changed her mind. She'd go with them to the rodeo after all.

"Wear those tight black jeans," Crissy said. "Do you have cowboy boots?"

"You know I don't."

"Okay, but wear some kind of boot, would you?" Then she squealed. "I can't believe you're going out with James. Finally!"

"It's not really a date, Crissy."

"Of course it is. We'll pick you up by seven."

Ashleigh hung up, knowing she was making a mistake. She didn't want to go. She knew she'd have no fun. It was Friday night. More often than not, Gina would bring pizza over and they'd watch a movie. And she'd ask Gina to stay over.

She glanced at her bed. Gina would call her mother, letting her know she was spending the night. She didn't know why they bothered with formalities. They both knew—as did their parents—that Gina wouldn't be going home. And during the night, after everyone else had gone to bed and the house was quiet, they'd stop pretending they were sleeping. They'd touch, they'd kiss...they'd make love.

Yet tonight, she'd let her mother talk her into going out on a stupid date. Truth was, she was afraid her mother was getting suspicious of all the time she and Gina spent together. It was actually a miracle they hadn't been caught yet.

She picked up the phone, dreading her call to Gina. Gina would be hurt. No, Gina would be confused. *And* hurt.

"Hi, Mrs. Granbury, it's Ashleigh. Is Gina around?"

"Hi, Ashleigh. Yes, she's out playing basketball with Jeff.

Hang on, I'll go get her."

"Thanks." She waited only a minute or two before Gina's breathless voice sounded in her ear.

"Hi. What's up?" Then softer, quieter, "I can't wait to see you."

Ashleigh bit her lip, not knowing how to tell her. "I'm going out tonight," she blurted. "With James." There was only silence on the other end and she waited.

"I see." A long pause, then, "Why?"

"My mother, she's been after me to date, she's starting to question why we spend so much time together. I thought—"

"Okay. I understand."

"Do you?"

"Yes. As long as we continue to hide what we have, what we feel, then yeah, your mother is going to wonder why you're not dating."

Ashleigh listened to her words but she was more interested in her tone. "You're mad," she finally stated.

"Yeah. Wouldn't you be?"

Ashleigh pulled the phone away from her ear as Gina slammed it down, effectively hanging up on her. She took a deep breath. Yeah, she'd be pissed if Gina called and said she had a date. In fact, she'd be mad as hell.

So what were you thinking?

Ashleigh plopped down on her bed, confused as to what to do. Well, she knew what she *should* do. She should call Crissy and cancel. But then she'd have some explaining to do to both Crissy and her mother. And then she'd most likely spend the night alone anyway as she doubted Gina—explanation or not—would want to come over.

"Crap. Shit. *Fuck*."

"Oh, man, you look great."

Yeah, she did. But James wasn't really the one she wanted to look great for. And after the argument with her mother—after she'd told her she *wasn't* going out with James—she was in no

85

mood for compliments. She obviously didn't win the argument with her mother.

Crissy pulled her aside, squeezing tightly on her arm. "What is *wrong* with you? You've got a pissed off look on your face."

Ashleigh ignored her question. "What are we doing here? I thought we were going to the rodeo?"

Crissy winked. "Well, James was so excited that you'd finally agreed to go out with him, he wanted to come by The Spot and show off."

Ashleigh glanced around. The Burger Spot was *the* place in town to go if you wanted to mingle with the cool kids. It was a teenager's dream, filled with video games and arcades, air hockey and foosball and lots of fun and laughter. It was where they gathered after Friday night football games, where they hung out on lazy Saturday afternoons or where they met up after school for a bitch or gossip session before heading home. And it was a place Ashleigh and Gina had avoided of late, choosing instead to spend their time alone.

"Crissy, I wouldn't really call this a date."

"Oh, my God, of course it is." Crissy pulled her back toward their booth. "And I think we're going to skip the rodeo and catch a movie instead."

"A movie?"

"Yeah." Crissy grinned and wiggled her eyebrows. "We can sit in the balcony and make out."

Ashleigh slid into the booth beside James, cringing as he spread his legs, his thigh pressing tightly against hers. She moved away from him.

"Burger and fries?" he asked. "My treat, of course."

She jumped when she felt his hand move across her leg to her inner thigh. "What the hell do you think you're doing?" she demanded as she slapped at his hand.

"Hey, I was just—"

"Well, don't," she said as she slid away, standing. "You don't touch me. Ever."

She spun away, hearing Crissy call her name. She ignored her as she headed to the back.

Stupid. Stupid.

She fished in her purse for coins, her hands shaking as she picked up the pay phone.

"Ashleigh? What is *wrong* with you?"

"Leave me alone, Crissy," she said, turning her back to her. *Please answer*. She knew Gina's parents were out. They went out to dinner every Friday night. But what if Gina wasn't home? What if—?

"Hello," came the familiar voice on the phone.

Crissy tapped her on the shoulder. "Ashleigh? Seriously. James is—"

"Ashleigh? What's wrong?" Gina's voice sounded in her ear and it was like a lifeline. She turned to Crissy. "Please, go back to the table."

"You're acting really weird. Really, really weird," Crissy said before turning in a huff and leaving her.

"Ashleigh?"

Ashleigh squeezed her eyes tight. "I love you," she whispered.

There was a pause. "Where are you?"

"The Spot."

"Do you want me to—"

"Yes. I want to be with you. I'm sorry. This was—"

"I'll be there in five minutes."

Ashleigh hung up the phone, her chest feeling tight. *I love you.* She couldn't believe she'd just blurted it out like that. As many times as they were intimate, as much as they talked, they'd never said those words to each other. Their lovemaking was always guarded, calculated, planned. They had to be careful. They had to be quiet. They couldn't let anyone know. Yet there were so many times those words came to her—she wanted to shout them out—as Gina brought her to orgasm. So many times she wanted to say them, but was afraid. They were two girls having sex. Did *I love you* belong there?

Yes, it did, she decided. Because, deep in her heart, she was *madly* in love with Gina Granbury. And despite the aloof attitude Gina normally sported, she knew—deep in her heart—that Gina felt the same.

She bent her head back, staring at the ceiling as she took a deep breath, then released it slowly. How was she going to get out of here? The booth that Crissy and the gang occupied was only six feet from the door. It wasn't like she could escape unnoticed. And without a scene. So she eyed the kitchen. There was a back door.

You've lost your mind.

But she pushed through the swinging doors, smiling brightly as everyone in the kitchen turned their gaze her way.

"Back door?" she asked.

They all pointed in the same direction and she nearly ran, sidestepping the guy pulling a dripping pan of fries from the grease. She saw the exit sign and pushed through the door, taking deep breaths of fresh air.

True to her word, Gina pulled up in the old Toyota her parents had bought for her. It was bordering on jalopy status and she knew Gina was embarrassed to drive it. Still more often than not, she rode her bike to school.

As soon as the car was stopped, Ashleigh jerked open the door, then hesitated before getting inside. She owed Gina an apology, an explanation.

"I'm sorry—"

"Get in. We'll talk later."

Ashleigh did, not daring to look at Gina as she drove.

"My parents went to dinner over in Pleasanton. They won't be home for hours."

Ashleigh turned to her and their eyes met. She nodded, knowing that meant they would be alone...for hours. Alone. No parents asleep down the hall. No siblings who might barge into the bedroom without knocking. No need to be guarded, to be quiet. She felt her excitement grow and she reached across the console, her left hand sliding over Gina's leg, resting intimately between her thighs. She felt Gina tremble, heard her breath catch.

Ashleigh leaned back, letting her hand move deeper, pressing hard into Gina's hot center.

"I'm going to drive us off the road if you don't stop," Gina said, her voice thick with desire.

Ashleigh opened her mouth, her breath coming in short gasps as she felt the warm moisture pooling between Gina's thighs. She left her hand where it was, feeling Gina tighten around it. They had been lovers for months, yet there was one thing they had not experienced. Not for lack of desire, no. But as quiet as they had to be, Ashleigh knew she would not be able to remain silent if Gina made love to her with her mouth. Tonight she wouldn't have to be silent.

Gina pulled to a stop in her normal spot on the street and they hurried from the car, nearly running into the house. Gina took her hand, leading her through the living room and down the hall to her bedroom. She closed the door, leaving the light off.

They stood there together, hands still clasped, looking at each other in the shadows.

"Did you mean what you said?"

Ashleigh took a deep breath. "Yes." She felt Gina pull her closer and she went, slipping into her arms, their mouths finding each other in the darkness. She moaned, loving the way Gina kissed her.

"I want all of you tonight," Gina murmured against her lips, her hands tugging Ashleigh's blouse from her jeans. "All of you. Everything."

"I'm yours," she whispered, unbuttoning her blouse as Gina's hands unzipped her jeans. She was soon naked and they nearly ripped Gina's clothes off, both tugging down her shorts at the same time.

Gina pulled the covers back on the bed, then lay down, bringing Ashleigh with her. Ashleigh didn't hesitate as she settled between her legs, loving the feel of skin on skin as she rested her weight on Gina. But Gina flipped them over, pinning her to the bed, her mouth covering one aching nipple, her lips tugging at it, sucking it into her mouth.

"Gina...*God*...please," she murmured, grasping Gina's head and holding her tight against her breast. She opened her legs wider, giving Gina room, feeling the steady rhythm of Gina's hips as she ground into her. Gina's mouth moved to her other breast, her tongue teasing, flicking at her nipple, making Ashleigh ache with a desire she hardly understood. "*Please...*"

But Gina understood. She lifted her head, her dark gaze fiery hot. "I love you too," she whispered.

Ashleigh felt tears sting her eyes. She cupped Gina's face, pulling her up, their mouths meeting gently now, their kiss languid, slow. Ashleigh pulled away, meeting Gina's eyes, trying to convey how she felt. "I'm sorry about tonight. I never should—"

"Shhh. No. We'll talk about it later. I just want to love you. Will you let me? Will you let me do everything?" She brought her mouth to Ashleigh's ear, her tongue bathing it, making Ashleigh squirm. "I want my tongue inside you. Not just my fingers, but my tongue. Do you want that?"

Ashleigh moaned, afraid she would climax right then, just from Gina's words and the very skilled tongue that was still invading her ear. "Yes. *Yes*," she said. "I want that."

Gina's mouth left her ear, pausing to nibble at her neck before moving lower. Ashleigh was trembling and she was nearly embarrassed by the sounds coming from her. She wanted Gina to hurry, but she took her time, her mouth moving slowly over the breasts, then lower.

"Oh, *God*," Ashleigh murmured. "Please, Gina...hurry."

"We don't have to hurry," Gina said as her tongue left a wet trail across her belly.

Ashleigh lifted her hips, offering herself to Gina. "I can't wait any longer. Please...*do it*." If she sounded like she was begging, she didn't care. This was an act she'd dreamed of for so long, and it was about to become a reality.

She felt Gina's mouth move across the hollow of her hips, nipping at the sensitive flesh of her inner thighs. Gina's hands pushed her legs farther apart, then Gina cupped her hips, holding her tight as she lowered her mouth.

"Oh...my...*God*," Ashleigh moaned, her hips jerking wildly as Gina's tongue moved into her wetness, delving inside her, licking across her clit, teasing her, then lips closing over her as Gina suckled her clit, much like she'd done her nipple earlier. "Gina ...oh, *God*, it feels so good," she panted. "So *good*. Please don't stop. Don't ever stop."

Gina didn't. With her mouth, she devoured Ashleigh—licking and sucking—holding her tight as Ashleigh writhed beneath her, totally out of control of both her mind and her body. Her fists held tight to the sheets as she struggled to breathe. The pleasure was immense and she let it wash over her, consume her, control her. Her orgasm came much too quickly, but she was powerless to stop it. Her scream was loud, she knew, but she couldn't help it. It felt so good to release it, to finally be free to express the pleasure Gina gave her. Her hips bucked as she came, and she clasped her thighs tight, holding Gina's mouth to her as her orgasm slowly subsided.

She finally lay limp, her body exhausted—sated. She smiled as Gina kissed her way up her body. She found the strength to gather her close, pulling Gina into her arms.

"That was *incredible*," she whispered. "I can't wait to do that to you."

CHAPTER SEVENTEEN

Present Day

Gina finally escaped Crissy's clutches, but not until Crissy had embarrassed both her and James Simpson. For all of his lovesick actions in high school, she would swear he was gay.

She found Ashleigh at the bar, standing alone, a flushed look on her face. She made her way over, Ashleigh turning to look at her as she got nearer. Gina nearly stumbled, the look in Ashleigh's eyes so familiar to her. It was the look she always had after they made love. Her eyes hooded, the blue made darker by her desire. As they stared, she saw a blush cover Ashleigh's face before she turned away.

But Gina's curiosity was piqued. She stood beside her, leaning on the bar as Ashleigh was doing, their arms brushing.

"Gonna share."

"What do you mean?"

"I've seen that look in your eyes before. Hundreds of times," she whispered.

Ashleigh laughed. "Hundreds, huh?"

"At least."

Ashleigh cleared her throat. "I'm embarrassed to say, but I took a trip down memory lane," she admitted.

Gina nudged her arm. "Share."

"Do you remember the night my mother talked me into going out with James? The night he tried to cop a feel at The Spot?"

Gina nodded. "I was pissed at you. And very hurt."

"Yes. I called you. You came to my rescue."

Gina turned to her. "You told me you loved me. It was the first time you said those words."

Ashleigh smiled. "Yes. That night was a first for a couple of things."

Gina tilted her head, trying to recall what happened. She picked Ashleigh up at The Spot and brought her home. Her parents were out late and they were alone. Oh...that was the night...

She smiled wickedly. "So, you were thinking about the first time I went down on you?"

Ashleigh blushed anew and lifted her empty glass to the bartender, silently asking for another. "I did not start out thinking about that. I was thinking about James, actually, and Crissy playing matchmaker."

"What do you remember about that night?" Gina asked quietly. It was a night she'd not thought of in years, yet it was one that held special meaning for her. Not the fact that they'd finally experimented with oral sex. No. But it was the night they said their first "I love you" to each other.

"If you think I'm going to discuss our past sex life, you're crazy as hell," Ashleigh said.

Gina smiled. "I had the most intense orgasm of my life that night. When your mouth touched me, I thought I was in heaven."

Ashleigh bumped her shoulder. "You *were* in heaven," she said with a laugh.

"But you know what I remember most?"

Ashleigh raised her eyebrows.

"I remember the look in your eyes when I told you I loved you." Gina swallowed. "It was the first time we were truly alone, the first time it wasn't just hurried sex, the first time we made love."

"Yes," Ashleigh whispered. "And after that, sneaking off for a quickie just didn't do it for us any longer."

Gina nodded. "Thank goodness for your grandparents' place."

Ashleigh sighed. "I can't believe we're discussing this. Actually, I can't believe we're speaking at all."

"What? You thought I'd still be upset and not want to talk to you? I'm over that, Ashleigh."

"*You'd* still be upset? What about me? Didn't you think I might possibly be upset?"

"Are we going to get into that again?"

"Yes. What did you mean earlier when you referred to the girl I was seeing?" She stepped away as the bartender brought over a new drink for her. "Thanks."

"I don't remember her name," Gina said, shaking her head at the bartender's unspoken question. She'd had enough alcohol for one night.

"*Who?* I never dated anyone. After we broke up, I was too devastated to date." She bumped Gina's shoulder again. "Not that you had that problem."

Gina pushed away from the bar. "I was devastated too, Ashleigh," she said quietly. "You broke my heart."

"Gina—"

Gina held up her hand, stopping her. "Let's don't get into it tonight, Ashleigh. I'm suddenly very tired. I think I'm going to call it a night."

"Okay. You're right. I don't suppose rehashing it will make any difference."

Gina nodded. "I'll see you at the pool party tomorrow."

She left Ashleigh standing at the bar, a confused look on her face. No, it wouldn't make any difference to rehash it all. All that would accomplish would be to dig up old memories, ones that were best left buried.

CHAPTER EIGHTEEN

Present Day

"Oh, my God!" Crissy stood, then shrieked again. "Oh, my *God*. Look at you."

Ashleigh's gaze was pulled from her book, following Crissy's movements. *Oh, my God, indeed.* Gina strode toward them, her bikini covered with a sheer white swim shirt, hiding nothing. Absolutely nothing. She was tanned a golden brown, evidence of her days on the beach. Her legs were as long as Ashleigh remembered, the muscles tight, defined. Runner's legs.

"What? Too old for a bikini?" Gina asked as the two women stared at her.

"You look fabulous." Crissy turned to Ashleigh and pointed. "And here I thought Ashleigh would be the only one to pull off wearing a bikini."

Ashleigh felt her face blush as Gina's eyes moved over her. There was nothing casual about her gaze and Ashleigh was conscious of Gina's prolonged stare at her breasts.

"You're as beautiful as ever," Gina said, her voice low.

Ashleigh smiled. "Thank you. You look stunning." She was pleased at the quick blush that covered Gina's face.

"Take my chair," Crissy said. "I need to help Brian get started." She walked away, then paused, looking back at them. "Look at you. I can't believe you're both single. We've got to fix that," she said as she left them.

"Single? She doesn't know about Faith?"

Ashleigh looked away. "I suppose not." *No, no one knew about Faith. Faith didn't even know about Faith.* She hid her smile, wondering if she should just tell Gina the truth. There was no Faith. Of course, how silly would that make her look? Then she'd have to confess as to why she made her up in the first place.

"Why didn't you bring her?"

Yes, why, Ashleigh? She forced a smile to her face. "She's never been here," she said truthfully. "It would be boring."

"Have you ever brought any of your lovers home to meet your parents?"

Ashleigh shook her head. "No. I don't make it back here all that often. Holidays and such."

"Oh? Crissy made it sound like you come five or six times a year."

As usual, Crissy talks too damn much. "What about you?"

"My first time back, believe it or not. You remember my parents moved to San Antonio shortly after we started college."

"That's right. And your dad died suddenly. I'm sorry."

"We had grown so far apart, especially after they divorced."

"Was it bitter?" She laughed. "Well, you know what I mean. I don't suppose any divorce is a cakewalk."

"It wasn't really bitter because it's what they both wanted. I didn't realize how miserable they were, I guess. But they went their separate ways and I was kinda left in the middle." She shrugged. "Totally blew them away when I came out to them."

"Yeah, mine too. But they recovered quickly."

"And your mom never suspected us? Even after you came out?"

"No. Not that she's ever mentioned, anyway. Yours?"

"Oh, yeah. First thing." Gina laughed. "My mom blamed you, because you know, good Catholic girls like me wouldn't ever cross that line."

"If she only knew how many lines you crossed," Ashleigh said.

Gina sighed. "Yeah, I did. Too many."

She suddenly had a sad look on her face and Ashleigh wondered what she was thinking of. She also wondered if Gina was ever going to want to talk about their breakup. Because she had questions and needed answers. Maybe if she had some sort of closure to the nagging questions she'd had all these years, well, then maybe she could go on with her life. Maybe she could finally let go of the past. Of course, that would be admitting that her life—her love life, at least—had been on hold. Not something she wanted to admit...or acknowledge. At least not to Gina. Because after all, there was Faith to think about. But to herself, she could readily accept the fact that no one ever touched her the way Gina had. Touched her physically nor emotionally. Even now, with twenty years behind them, she could still feel that spark, still feel the power between them. She wondered if Gina felt it too.

"Why did you break up with me?" Ashleigh whispered.

Gina turned, her eyes filled with reflection and sadness. "I wanted to give you your freedom."

"Why? Because you wanted yours?"

"No. I never wanted anyone but you."

Ashleigh turned away, embarrassed by the jealousy she still felt. "Yet you slept with countless girls, night after night?"

"I was trying to forget you. I was trying to get you out of my heart, out of my head. It was the only way I could cope. I'm sorry."

"Gina, I never wanted my freedom. I never understood why you did that."

"I didn't want you to have to sneak around, Ashleigh. You didn't deserve that. If I wasn't the one, then—"

"What the hell are you talking about? That's the third or

fourth time you've alluded to that. Did you think there was someone else?"

"I saw you with her, Ashleigh. It was twenty years ago, so there's no need to pretend any longer."

As much as she wanted to discuss this, to *know*...Ashleigh was too furious to continue the conversation in a rational tone. "You're driving me fucking insane with these insinuations. Let's just get it out and quit talking in goddamn circles," she said, her voice rising.

Gina grinned. "Wow, you did develop a potty mouth, didn't you?" She stood and ripped off her swim shirt, leaving her standing there practically naked. "I don't want to talk about it right now." She strode the few feet to the pool and dove in, making barely a splash.

Ashleigh stared, her eyes glued to the sleek figure as she glided under the surface. It wasn't fair. Not after twenty years. She should be over it by now. But damn if she didn't feel that old attraction rearing its ugly head. She sighed. And who was this mystery girl Gina kept alluding to?

Gina was surprised by the sudden splashing around her as she surfaced. Apparently, all it had taken was for her to get in the pool to get the others to follow. She looked around, seeing somewhat familiar faces but not a single name would come to her. And while she was friendly enough in high school, she realized that Ashleigh was really the only true friend she had. The others were just classmates, faces in the crowd, kids she saw every single day, yet knew hardly anything about them. Ashleigh's friends had welcomed her into their circle—Crissy, Jennifer, the guys—but only because Ashleigh insisted. She had nothing in common with them. They all came from prominent families who purchased brand-new sports cars for them, and most lived on the newer north side of town, complete with two-story houses and pools in the backyards, Ashleigh included. However, being madly in love did tend to make one overlook some things.

"Having fun?"

She spun around, surprised to find Ashleigh in the pool beside her. She smiled. "I don't know any of these people."

"At the dance tonight, we'll wear nametags. That should help."

Gina moved closer, teasing. "Do you think anyone would be shocked if the two lesbians danced together?"

"Shocked only in that no one knows you're gay," Ashleigh said.

"As much of a tomboy as I was in high school, and now here I am, not married," she shrugged. "Come on, who wouldn't at least guess?"

"Well, if you're just dying to out yourself to everyone, I'll be happy to dance with you."

Gina playfully splashed water at her. "I don't think we've ever danced together, have we?"

"Well, we danced the night of the prom. Remember?"

"Oh, yes. You were beautiful. The dance didn't last long, if I recall."

"Then there was the night out at my grandparents' pond where you sang to me while we danced."

Gina couldn't resist as she moved closer, nearly pinning Ashleigh to the side of the pool. "Isn't that the night we got very adventurous and tried to—"

Ashleigh covered Gina's mouth with her hand and grinned. "Don't you dare say that out loud."

"I think I pulled a hamstring, didn't I?"

Ashleigh laughed. "How did we ever come up with that idea?"

"You were on your period, but you didn't want to waste an opportunity—"

Again, a wet hand covered her mouth. "I remember. You don't have to say it. But I think I enjoyed the prom dance more."

"Me too." Gina moved away, enjoying being near Ashleigh far more than she should. "I think we would have died if not for your grandparents' place though."

"I know. And honestly, I can't go out there without..."

"Thinking about us being together?" Gina finished for her.
"Yes."

"Are they still alive?"

Ashleigh shook her head. "No. They've been gone years now. They died eight months apart. They had four children, so the place and the land was supposed to be divided, but no one really wanted that and no one wanted to buy from the others. They ended up keeping it together, just selling enough acres to have money to remodel the house and put in a pool. None of my mother's siblings live near here, so when they come, they usually stay at least a week. It's turned into quite the vacation getaway. And it's where we do Christmas each year. It's a shame it took them dying to bring everybody together."

"But your mom has the upkeep on it?"

"Yes. After a big weekend, they'll just hire someone to clean it, but the pool has turned into the biggest headache. My father hates it. That's his chore to keep it clean."

Gina dipped her head into the water, then slicked her hair back from her face. "And how are Mark and Courtney?"

Ashleigh leaned closer. "Mark is a big flaming queen and lives in San Francisco. Courtney is a gynecologist and she's in San Antonio."

Gina burst out laughing, causing those around them to turn and stare. "Mark is a queen?"

"He pretends to be bi so mom and dad can still hold out hope for marriage, but yeah, he's a big homo."

"And Courtney is a gynecologist? Wow, lucky gal," Gina said with a grin.

"Perhaps a profession you should have gone into," Ashleigh teased. "Speaking of which, what did you end up doing?"

"Advertising."

"Really?"

Gina took Ashleigh's hand and pulled her into deeper water, away from the others. They were bouncing on their toes, necks just above water. "Remember how I liked to draw?"

"Yes, you used to sketch all the time. I thought you'd be an

101

artist. You had the temperament for one."

"Funny."

"Sorry. Go on."

"Well, I never really knew what I wanted to do. I was just taking classes, hoping something jumped out at me. Tracy talked me into taking some marketing classes. I got introduced to advertising there. But the business side of things didn't interest me like the design did. I got a job doing ad design in Austin at one of the top firms and I was happy enough there."

"Collecting a paycheck without a whole lot of responsibility?"

"Pretty much. But my personal life sucked," she admitted. She saw the questions in Ashleigh's eyes but she wasn't prepared to admit that she was still trying to chase Ashleigh's memory away at the time. "That's when I ran into Tracy and took a trip down to Corpus. I fell in love with the place. Tracy worked for a marketing firm and got me a job, but it was just a job. Nothing I enjoyed, certainly. One night I was over at their house for steaks and while Sammy—that's her husband—was doing the cooking, we were downing a couple of bottles of wine. We decided to start our own advertising agency."

"Oh, wow. That's wonderful."

Gina moved, guiding them back into the shallow water again. "Yeah. A few lean years at the beginning, though. But we're doing good now. We actually have enough business to employ another designer, so I'm not strapped with it all. Tracy pretty much handles the accounts and business side of things. It's worked out good for us."

"That's great. You love your job now, right?"

"Yeah. I can't see myself doing anything else. What about you?"

"Oh, no. I hate my job."

"The attorney part or the job part?"

"Both. Unfortunately, I'm very good at what I do and they pay me accordingly. Our firm specializes in the oil and gas industry."

"Oh, no."

"Yes. I'm afraid so."

"What's your specialty?"

"Loopholes."

"Writing them or finding them?"

"Both."

"Wow. Carly would hate you."

"Carly?"

"She's a wildlife biologist. She and Pat run a private sanctuary down close to Aransas. She's always fighting with your oil and gas folks over drilling rights, environmental protections, things like that."

"Friends of yours?"

"Yeah. Pat has a beach house in Port Aransas. I actually met her jogging one morning."

Ashleigh made a face. "You jog?"

"Yes. I still bike some too, but mostly take a run."

"I hate running. My workout partner loves it. We trade off. I prefer to bike."

Gina laughed. "So this weekend, you aren't going to hit the trails."

"There are no trails in Calloway." She moved closer. "But tell me about your friends."

"Pat and Carly? They're crazy in love. They're my closest gay friends, although I don't get to see them that often. From my place in Corpus to the refuge is over an hour and a half drive. I get out there probably twice a month or so, depending on the season. Sometimes they're too busy. Spring and early summer are nearly impossible to get together."

"What does Pat do?"

"She's a photographer. Does awesome work." Gina reached out and brushed a water droplet from Ashleigh's face. She was surprised by the darkening of Ashleigh's eyes. "Beautiful," she whispered. "I had forgotten how brilliant your eyes are. Like an indigo bunting."

"A what?" Ashleigh asked, her voice low.

"A bird. A tiny little blue bird. They migrate through by the thousands."

Ashleigh smiled. "You're a bird-watcher? Seriously?"

Gina laughed. "Hardly. Only what I've learned from Carly. I'm kinda like Pat. She's an extremely talented wildlife photographer, but she couldn't name a bird to save her life." Gina was surprised to feel Ashleigh's hand touch her arm, even more surprised to feel her fingers wrap around it.

"You've changed. You seem much more introspective."

"You mean as opposed to an eighteen-year-old obsessed with sneaking off and having sex with you?" Gina pulled herself out of the pool and sat along the edge, her legs dangling in the water. She looked down at Ashleigh. "Or were you referring to my antics in college?"

"Both, I guess." Ashleigh moved closer, standing between her legs. "I really need to talk about that, Gina. I've hated you all these years and I don't want to hate you. But I was just left with so many questions." Gina felt the fluttering of her stomach as Ashleigh's hands clasped around each of her ankles. "Can we please talk about it? Please?"

Gina wasn't sure what it would accomplish to talk about their past, but obviously they had two different versions of their breakup. Because in all honesty, Gina had hated Ashleigh, too, all these years. But the woman she saw now wasn't the young teen she'd fallen in love with, and she wasn't the girl who had broken her heart either. Ashleigh had grown into a beautiful, confident woman. And much like the young teen she'd been, she was still able to turn questions into commands...ones Gina was never able to refuse.

"Okay. We'll talk. How about after hot dogs, we take a drive?" Gina suggested.

"Thank you."

CHAPTER NINETEEN

Twenty years ago

"What's your hurry?"

"You know what my hurry is," Ashleigh said, ignoring the slower pace Cheryl tried to set.

"Oh, yeah, you haven't seen her in like three hours," Cheryl teased. "However did you stand it?"

Ashleigh grinned. "I'm in love. I can't help it."

"I can't believe you two have been sleeping together since high school and you still have the hots for each other. It's crazy."

"Not crazy. We're going to be together forever."

"Yeah, right."

"We are," Ashleigh insisted. Why wouldn't they? She and Gina were perfect for each other. Best friends and lovers. They never argued. They talked and laughed and made love. She took a deep breath. Boy, did they make love.

"There's tall, dark and beautiful now," Cheryl said. "I'll catch up with you this afternoon. And hey, thanks for talking with me earlier."

"Yeah, okay," Ashleigh said, but her eyes were already locked on Gina. Something was wrong. There was sadness in her eyes that Ashleigh had never seen before. She waited for her, searching her eyes. "What's wrong?" she asked.

"We need to talk," Gina said. She shifted her feet nervously, then shoved both hands into the pockets of her jeans.

"Okay, but what's wrong. Did something happen? You look so sad. Did someone—"

"Come here," Gina said, pulling her to the side, away from the sidewalk as students rushed by on their way to class.

"Gina, you're scaring me."

"I've been...I've been thinking," she said. "We're so young. We haven't really, you know, had an opportunity to get to know other people. I think—"

Ashleigh grabbed her arm and squeezed. "What the hell are you talking about?"

"Maybe we need to take a break."

"Take a break?"

"Hang out with other people for awhile. You know..."

Ashleigh dropped her arm. "You want to break up?" she whispered. Her chest was so tight she could hardly breathe. "Is that what you're saying?"

"Yeah. You know, we're young. We should...branch out. Experience life."

Ashleigh couldn't contain her tears any longer. "Are you serious? You want to be with someone else? You want to *sleep* with someone else?"

"Ashleigh, I'm doing this for you," Gina said. "Please don't cry."

"You're doing this for me? Well, that's just bullshit," she said, her voice loud. "What happened, Gina? We were together last night. You told me you loved me. We made love last night and you said you loved me. Suddenly today, you want to break up?"

Gina took her hands and held them tightly. "I *do* love you," she whispered. "And I want you to be happy. And I want you to be able to do what you want." She stepped away and Ashleigh saw she was fighting her own tears. "I'll never forget you."

Ashleigh was speechless as she watched Gina walk away... walk away and out of her life.

CHAPTER TWENTY

Present Day

"I never would have pictured you for a Bimmer," Gina said. "At least not a sedan. Maybe a ragtop."

"I just bought it last year." Ashleigh grinned. "BMW is not really my style. I had a truck before that."

"My, aren't you the lesbian," Gina teased.

"Right." Actually, Ashleigh could play the girlie-girl when the occasion called for it, but she liked being the *sporty* lesbian, something she wasn't when she was younger.

"I can't believe how much Calloway has changed."

"I know. Past our hotel, it's really crazy. It's almost like another town."

"But we're heading where?"

"I thought you'd like to see the old high school," she said.

Gina raised an eyebrow. "What do you mean old?"

"It's a middle school now. They built a new high school a few years ago." Ashleigh turned off the highway and slowed, going down the old strip. "Remember that?" she asked, pointing.

"The Burger Spot. Damn, is it still open?"

"Yeah. But since the high school moved, it's not the hangout like it was when we were here."

"It was never really my hangout anyway," Gina said. "I wasn't one of the *cool* kids."

"Only because you didn't want to be."

Gina laughed. "Neither did you."

"No. I only wanted to be with you," she admitted.

Gina nodded. "And vice versa."

Ashleigh took a deep breath as she turned down the street where the old high school had been. The building was the same, but it appeared much smaller now. She drove around the back where the practice fields used to be.

"A baseball field?"

"It's not the school's. They built a new field up north. This used to be the practice field, remember?"

"Of course I remember. There was a lovely hidden spot behind the bleachers. We used to—"

Ashleigh laughed. "I *know* what we used to do there." She pulled to a stop. "This field is used for Little League mostly." She opened the door. "You want to walk around?"

"Sure."

They were silent as they walked past the baseball field and headed to the tennis courts. They appeared to be the same courts that were there twenty years ago, the surface showing signs of age as cracks snaked through the concrete. Ashleigh stopped, ready to talk.

"Tell me why."

Gina looked past her, her gaze going to the old school. Ashleigh wondered if she was thinking about the breakup or taking a trip down memory lane, remembering their time together here in this building.

"I knew you had another lover," Gina said finally. "I was trying to spare you from having to sneak around."

Ashleigh frowned. "What the *hell* are you talking about?"

Gina shrugged. "I don't remember her name. Some cute little short chick. Blond. You had a class together. You went to lunch nearly every day with her."

Ashleigh had tried to erase that time from her memory so she had a hard time recalling anyone she knew back then. "Cheryl?"

"Yeah. I think that was her name."

Ashleigh felt her anger surface. "You thought I was sleeping with Cheryl? That's why you broke up with me?"

"Look, I didn't believe it at first, but people kept telling me it was true." Gina paused. "So one day I waited for you after your class...I saw you together."

"Together? You're out of your mind. Cheryl was crazy about ...oh, what was her name?" Ashleigh closed her eyes, trying to remember. "Amanda something or other. I was trying to give her pointers, trying to help her, trying to get her to ask Amanda out. When she finally did, it didn't go well."

"Amanda? Who do you think first told me about you and Cheryl? It was Amanda. They were best friends."

"*What?* Are we talking about the same Amanda?"

Gina walked closer. "Amanda told me right where you'd be, what time, everything. And there you were. You were hugging. Then she pulled you to the side near some shrubs, and you kissed and hugged again." Gina shook her head. "Wasn't just a friendly hug, Ashleigh. It was a full body *I'm about to jump your bones* hug."

Ashleigh clenched her fists, surprised at her anger. "You have *got* to be kidding me. You broke up with me because someone told you I was sleeping with Cheryl? Did you ever think to ask me?" Ashleigh poked Gina's chest with her finger. "God, your communication skills always did suck." She turned away. "I was so in love with you, I never even looked at another girl, much less entertained the idea of sleeping with one." She turned back to Gina, holding her eyes. "You were my world. I loved you," she whispered. "And I was floored when you came to me with your little speech about needing to see others, needing to spread our wings, needing to experience life. I was devastated. I thought I

110

was going to die. Hell, I wanted to die." She took a step back, away from Gina. "Every time I turned around, you were with someone else. And I hated you. I hated you so much."

"Ashleigh, look, I'm sorry if—"

"No. I'm so pissed at you right now, I don't want to talk to you." She spun around and headed back to the car, her pulse pounding so fast, so loud, she was afraid she might have a stroke right there. *She thought I was cheating on her?* "Fucking unbelievable," she muttered.

"Ashleigh, wait."

"For what? Wait for what?" She stopped, glaring at Gina. "Why couldn't you talk to me about it? Why couldn't you ask me? You ended our relationship based on a *rumor?*" She took a deep breath, trying to curb her anger. "Were you that insecure about us, about our relationship?"

"Ashleigh, you were a cheerleader. You were popular. Your parents gave you a brand-new sports car when you turned sixteen." Gina looked away. "I came from the south side of town. My parents got me a beat-up Toyota when I was seventeen. I—"

"You didn't think you were good enough?" Ashleigh's anger disappeared as fast as it had come. She finally understood. "I'm sorry." She walked closer, pulling Gina into her arms and holding her tight. "I should have seen that. But you of all people should have known that none of that mattered to me."

"She drove a Corvette. She—"

"Oh, Gina. She was hardly even a friend. You were my world. I fell in love with you. *You.* I didn't care who your parents were or where you lived. I didn't care what kind of car you drove. I never cared about any of that."

Gina looked away. "I was always awed by the thought that you wanted to be with me," she said. "You could have had anyone. Anyone in high school, certainly in college. So when Amanda said that Cheryl, the rich kid from Dallas, was sleeping with you—"

"You believed her."

"I believed her. I didn't at first, but it all added up. You had a couple of classes together. You went to lunch with her. You met up at the library. She called you all the time."

"Which is what people do when they have classes together and they study." She shook her head. "All these years I've tried to figure out why. I thought maybe I was lacking, maybe you had your eye on someone else. Hell, maybe you did want to spread your wings. God knows you slept with enough girls after us."

"I was stupid. I should have talked to you. But Amanda and Cheryl—"

"Set us up," Ashleigh finished for her. She saw it now. All the attention Cheryl used to pay her. All the touching, the impromptu hugs, the phone calls. Yes, she could see Gina getting suspicious.

Gina nodded. "Cheryl wanted you. It turns out Amanda wanted me."

Again, Ashleigh felt a stab of jealousy. "Well, at least one of them got their wish."

Gina grabbed her arm when she would have turned away. "I'm sorry, Ashleigh. You're right. My communication skills sucked. I was lost without you. And so I tried to forget you."

"By sleeping with everyone within—"

"Yes."

Ashleigh pulled away from her. "It was two years before I would let anyone touch me. And even then, it was a disaster." She laughed quietly. "I even tried guys, thinking...well, I don't know what I was thinking," she admitted. *Talk about disaster.*

"Guys?"

"I know. It was stupid." She looked away. No, what was stupid was that after twenty years, she was still trying to forget Gina. And her sexual encounters were still disastrous. Of course, there was Faith, she recalled, trying to find some humor in the situation. Good old Faith.

"So, do you hate me more or less now?"

Ashleigh tried to smile. "I'm not sure. Of course, I guess you were right about some things."

"What do you mean?"

"We were awfully young. We were the only partners either of us had ever had. I guess it was crazy to think we'd actually stay together. I mean, college and all. Chances are, we would have met someone else and ended up breaking up anyway."

Gina nodded. "We've both changed. I'm sure we would have grown apart."

"Yeah. Of course. And if I'd stayed at college there, I'd have been a teacher." She laughed. "Now that would have been a disaster."

"So see? It all worked out. You've got your job, your fancy office. You've got a partner in your life. I've got...I've got a thriving business and a small group of very good friends. And I love living on the coast." Gina shrugged. "See? It worked out."

"Did it?" she whispered. She had a job she hated and an imaginary lover she created so Gina wouldn't know she was still single. Gina at least had a job she loved, in a city she loved. But she too had no lover. Had it really worked out?

"Come on. We have a few hours before the shindig tonight. I'd love to see your mother."

"Mom?"

"Yeah. Do you think she'd mind?"

"No. No, she would love to see you." Ashleigh paused at the car. "Let me just call her. Make sure she's home."

"Okay. Great."

Ashleigh walked a few steps away from the car. Her mother answered on the second ring. "Hey, Mom. You remember Gina Granbury?"

"Of course, honey." Her mother laughed. "We just talked about her, didn't we?"

Ashleigh rolled her eyes. "Well, she's here. You know, for the reunion. She wants to see you. Do you mind if we drop by?" She glanced into the car, seeing Gina watching her.

"Oh, good. Bring her by. It'll be nice to see her again."

Ashleigh cleared her throat. "Okay...and just so you know, I've been seeing Faith for, well, for the last several years."

"Who?"

Ashleigh bit her lip. "Faith." She glanced back to Gina, hoping she couldn't hear.

113

"Faith? Well why haven't you brought her around?"

"Mom, just work with me here, okay?"

"You're seeing someone and you don't even bother to let us know."

"*Mother*...just go with me, okay. Jesus. How hard is it?"

"What are you talking about?"

Ashleigh sighed. "We'll be right over."

"Wow. So many memories here," Gina said as she stared at the house.

"Did you go by your old place?"

She shook her head. "No. My own house was so sterile. My dad was gone all the time. My mom, well, I don't know what she did. But here, here it was a normal house, with kids and laughter. I love the time I spent here."

Ashleigh led the way up the walk. "Yes, nearly every weekend."

"Yeah. Fighting for pizza with Mark and Courtney. Then going to your room and locking the door." She grinned. "And then—"

"I remember exactly what happened. We don't need to go there."

Gina laughed. "So I shouldn't tell your mother?"

"That we were having sex two doors down from them? Let's don't." She knocked once, then opened the front door. "Mom?"

"In the kitchen, honey."

"It doesn't look the same," Gina said as they went toward the kitchen. "Didn't there used to be a wall there?"

"Yes. She likes to redecorate, remodel, change things around. I'm surprised they haven't just sold and built a new house as much as she likes change."

Her mother smiled broadly when she saw Gina, immediately pulling her into a hug. "Oh, my goodness, look at you," she said. "You're absolutely beautiful, Gina. My, my, but you turned out to be a looker."

Ashleigh laughed at the blush Gina now sported. But Gina

recovered quickly, kissing her mother on the cheek.

"You look as lovely as I remember, Mrs. Pence."

"Oh, you're too kind. But you always were a charmer. Wasn't she, Ashleigh?"

Ashleigh's eyes flew to Gina's. What did she mean by that comment? But she nodded, "Yes, she was a charmer, all right."

"I made us some refreshments. Let's go out to the patio. It's not so terribly hot today."

Ashleigh eyed the pitcher. "I forgot to tell you," she said to Gina. "My mother has turned into an afternoon lush."

Her mother laughed and waved her hand dismissively. "Call it what you want, honey, but your father likes it." She poured three glasses. "He says it makes me wild."

It was Ashleigh's turn to blush. "We didn't need to know that."

"Sex after sixty is quite good, Ashleigh."

"And we *really* didn't need to know that." She picked up one of the glasses, then motioned to the patio. "Shall we?"

They settled under the ceiling fan on the patio and Ashleigh watched as Gina surveyed the backyard, her gaze landing on the pristine pool. She wondered if Gina remembered the nights they'd sneak down after everyone was asleep. They'd shed their clothes and slip into the dark end of the pool...touching, kissing. And sometimes, when the kissing and touching wasn't enough, Gina would lead her from the pool into the shadows, making love to her as Ashleigh struggled to stand, struggled to keep quiet as she climaxed.

She caught Gina's eye, holding her gaze, knowing she was reliving the same memories as Ashleigh.

"Tell me what you've been up to, Gina," her mother coaxed. "I run into Lou every once in a while. She says you're down in Corpus."

"Yes. I've been there several years now. I love it down there. I should thank you for allowing me to go on vacation with you way back when. That was my first introduction to the coast."

"That's funny how that worked out, isn't it? I don't believe

Ashleigh has been back down there since you two were seniors."

"Really?" Gina looked at her. "Why not?"

"Well, I've just been busy," she said. She sipped from her drink, hoping they weren't expecting more of an explanation.

"Yes. I suppose when you're in a relationship, you have to take the other person into account. Does she not like the coastal area?"

Her mother frowned. "She who?"

"Faith," Gina said.

"Oh, yes, *Faith*. Of course, we've never met her. You'd think—"

"Mother," Ashleigh said sternly, "Gina doesn't want to hear about Faith."

Gina leaned forward. "I'd love to hear about her. I'm wondering what kind of woman finally captured your heart."

"Yes, so would I," her mother said.

Ashleigh felt her face turn red and she picked up her glass again quickly. "I don't care to discuss my love life in front of my mother, thank you very much."

"So you've not met her?" Gina asked her mother, ignoring her.

"No. In fact, just today is the first I've heard of her."

"Oh, good God," Ashleigh said. "Can we talk about something else?" She grabbed the bridge of her nose and squeezed. Inventing Faith was a mistake, no doubt. But bringing Gina over to see her mother? *What were you thinking?* She drained the last of her margarita and held up the glass. "Who wants seconds?"

"My, talk about a lush," her mother murmured.

CHAPTER TWENTY-ONE

Present Day

Gina stood naked in her room, eyeing the clothes she'd laid out on the bed. While the dinner and dance wasn't deemed formal, Crissy advised it was a dress-up affair. However, this was Calloway. Not all "dress-up" rules applied here. Especially if you weren't all that fond of dressing up in the first place.

The black jeans with the nice leather boots is what Gina wanted to wear. What she knew she should wear was the fancy suit Tracy had picked out for her. Would it be considered a fashion faux pas if she mixed the silky turquoise blouse of the suit with the tight black jeans? Gina decided she didn't care. She wasn't really a suit kind of gal. She was simply letting Tracy play dress-up with her when they'd gone shopping.

She glanced at her watch, knowing she had another half an hour before they were to meet at the bar for pre-dinner drinks. Then dinner and dancing. And a brunch tomorrow for those who wanted, then they would all disperse and go on with their lives. Of course, Gina hadn't spent much time talking to anyone other than Ashleigh and a few short conversations with Crissy. She'd had a brief—and awkward—encounter with Jennifer, the girl famous for her swim parties. Gina didn't recognize her as she was just a few ounces shy of three hundred pounds now. Divorced with two kids, she still lived in Calloway. That was the extent of their conversation and Gina escaped back to the safety of Ashleigh's company.

Which was ironic, seeing as how she'd been dreading meeting up with Ashleigh again. She couldn't believe they'd actually discussed the breakup. More than that, she was shocked by Ashleigh's claim that she and the cute little blonde hadn't been lovers. Oh, Gina believed her. Ashleigh had no reason to lie about it now. She just couldn't believe she'd let herself get set up like that, let herself believe it was true, let her insecurities catch up with her. Ashleigh claimed to have hated Gina all these years. Well, the feeling was mutual. Gina had lived with the thought that Ashleigh had cheated on her, had lived with the feeling that she wasn't quite good enough for Ashleigh, whether it be sex or whatever. All these years she believed that Ashleigh had found *her* lacking and had turned to someone else.

All these wasted years.

Well, at least Ashleigh had been able to finally move on. If she and Faith had been together a handful of years, then maybe she'd found her true love. It was odd though that she hadn't even introduced Faith to her parents.

Gina sighed. Yes, all these wasted years. She'd like to think that maybe now—now that they'd cleared the air about what had happened—she'd be able to move on and perhaps let someone into her life again, into her heart. Not that she'd been intentionally keeping them out, she just hadn't given anyone a fair chance. Because in the back of her mind, in the back of her heart, she was still comparing everyone she met with Ashleigh. She was still trying to find that magic she'd had with Ashleigh, even though she knew she'd probably never find it again.

Ashleigh stared at herself in the mirror, wondering if she dared to wear the black strapless dress or not. She had to admit it looked wonderful on her, clinging to her curves, the front cut low, revealing far too much cleavage for Calloway. She spun around, grinning at her reflection as the dress lifted, exposing her tanned thighs. Yeah, she dared.

Mainly because she wanted to see Gina's reaction.

But that was wrong, wasn't it? Because there was Faith. And what kind of message would that send?

I don't care.

Yes, truth was, she didn't care. Because there *wasn't* Faith. However, did she really want to play with fire and actually flirt with Gina? That could be very dangerous.

"Oh, hell," she muttered as she grabbed her cell. She was about to call Pam but put the phone down quickly. Why was she calling Pam for advice? Pam would encourage her, not try to talk some sense into her. "Why does she have to be single? And why does she have to be so damn gorgeous?"

CHAPTER TWENTY-TWO

Twenty years earlier

"You look beautiful, honey."

Ashleigh rolled her eyes as her mother surveyed her after hooking the string of pearls around her neck.

"So does this mean you and James are dating?"

"We're not dating, Mom. I just agreed to go to the prom with him, that's all." Another decision she was certain to regret but *not* going to the prom simply wasn't an option. She'd already been voted Miss Calloway and was in the running for prom Queen. She hoped her very public chagrin over the Miss Calloway title—and her insistence that she did not want the prom Queen title—would get everyone to vote for Crissy. In fact, she'd campaigned for Crissy.

"Is it true Gina's not going?"

Ashleigh bit her lip. "Yes."

"Did no one invite her? I find that hard to believe. She's such an attractive girl."

"She got invited. But the prom's not really her thing." No. It wasn't Ashleigh's thing, either. Yet here she was, dressed in a formal gown, wearing her grandmother's pearls, waiting for James Simpson to pick her up.

"I just can't understand how the two of you could go all through high school without having a boyfriend. It's just not normal. Everyone should want to go to their prom."

It was a theme of conversation that Ashleigh had been trying to avoid for the last two years. She'd made up countless excuses and reasons as to why she didn't have a boyfriend, but it still fell on deaf ears.

"So I should be like everyone else?" she asked. "I want to go to college and make something of my life. But you want me to date one of the boys here in Calloway because it's normal? You really want me having sex with any of these boys?"

"Who said anything about sex?"

"Well, what do you think happens on dates? They sneak off and have sex." Ashleigh couldn't believe she was talking to her mother like this. The last thing she wanted was to get into a conversation about sex. After all, they'd never really had the *sex* talk. And judging by the blush on her mother's face, they weren't going to have it now, either.

"So you're saving yourself for marriage. That's how it should be. I'm very proud of you."

Ashleigh hated lying to her mother. Saving herself for marriage? No, there would be no marriage. Not to a man, anyway. She and Gina were both heading to San Marcos for college. There, they could be themselves. They could be open with their relationship. They would meet others like them and not feel so isolated, so alone. No more sneaking off. No more lying.

That is, if she could get through the night. She'd made it plain to James that she was going with him as a friend, not as a date. And she'd already told Crissy that if he attempted *anything*, she would leave.

"Oh, my God. You look beautiful."

Ashleigh smiled at Crissy. "No, *you* look beautiful. You look like the prom queen," she said with a wink.

"Well, sorry, sweetie, but I heard through the grapevine that you and Brian won."

"Me and Brian? I hate this crap. I don't want to be the fucking prom queen," she protested, perhaps a bit too loudly.

"Look on the bright side. At least it wasn't James who won. He'd definitely think you two were a couple then."

"That's a bright side?"

"What's the big deal? You dance with Brian, take a few pictures, let everyone gape at you, smile like you love it. Easy as pie."

"I know you don't understand, but I can't do it." In fact, she was nearly in panic mode. She was so certain she'd done enough to get Crissy voted prom queen.

"You have to do it."

"The hell I do."

Crissy grabbed her arm as she turned to go. "You can't just leave. Have you lost your mind?"

"Why is this happening to me? I'm not a cheerleader anymore. I'm not supposed to win this crap. *You're* supposed to win."

"You're nice. They like you."

"*You're* nice," she said convincingly.

"I'm a snob." Crissy pulled her closer. "If you run away every time you go out with James, he's going to get a complex."

"That was a year ago."

"Exactly. And you haven't been out with him—or anyone else—since then." She paused as she stared across the room. "Oh, God, look at Jennifer. She's practically naked. Did she think wearing something like that would get Seth back?"

"Is she still hung up on him?"

"Yes. He's a loser."

Ashleigh rolled her eyes. Anyone who broke up with anyone in their group was labeled a *loser*. She was so ready for high school to be over. A few more months, then freedom. She and Gina could escape this little town and be together without having to pretend going to the prom was the best thing in the world. In fact, right now, she didn't care if James got a complex or not. She didn't care that her mother would be pissed. And she didn't care what any of her classmates thought. But she wasn't going to suffer through the pageantry of the naming of the prom king and queen and then the subsequent slow dance afterward. She wasn't going to do it.

"Look, I'm feeling sick. Nauseous," she clarified.

"You're not sick."

"Trust me, I'm sick. I'm going to vomit." She squeezed Crissy's arm. "I'll let James know, then I'm going to call my mother to come pick me up."

"She's going to be pissed."

"Not if I'm sick." She also knew her mother wasn't home. They'd gone over to the Parker's for dinner and cards. Mark and Courtney were sleeping over at a friend's house.

"I can't believe you're doing this."

"I'll let Mrs. Ashmore know, don't worry." Mrs. Ashmore held the crown jewels for the king and queen to wear after the announcement.

After a quick explanation to James—who then gallantly offered to take her home—and to Mrs. Ashmore—whose genuine dismay told Ashleigh she really did win—Ashleigh slipped into one of the offices to pretend to call her mother. She called Gina instead. Thankfully it was Gina who answered and not one of her parents.

"Can you come get me?"

"What's wrong?"

"I'm going to win stupid prom queen," she said.

"I told you so."

"So you did. Will you come get me?"

"Can you just leave like that?"

"I'm sick."

"Okay. My folks are here though," she said quietly.

Ashleigh smiled. "Mine aren't. Mark and Courtney are gone too."

123

"I'll be there in five minutes."

Ashleigh felt a thrill as she hung up the phone. She knew she looked good, knew the dress she wore clung to her curves. And she wanted nothing more than for Gina to see her in it. Actually, she wanted nothing more than for Gina to strip it off of her. She closed her eyes, wondering if she'd always feel this way, wondering if the thought of making love with Gina would always send chills across her body in anticipation. She decided that, yes, it would always be this way.

She went back out, but not before plastering a sickly, pathetic look on her face. Mrs. Ashmore was waiting.

"My parents aren't home. I forgot they were going out to dinner. I called Gina instead. She's going to take me home."

"Okay, dear. It's a shame Gina didn't come tonight. She's such a pretty girl. I heard that several of the boys asked her."

Ashleigh shrugged. "Gina plays basketball. I don't think she owns a dress."

Mrs. Ashmore laughed appropriately, then patted her arm. "Would you like me to wait with you?"

"No. She just lives about five minutes from here."

"Okay, dear. I hope you feel better." She looked around them conspiratorially before leaning closer. "I just wanted you to know that you won. Crissy was runner-up, so she'll get the traditional dance."

"Thank you. And if I felt any better, I'd stay for it, but I feel like I could throw up at any moment." She covered her mouth as if to prevent just that and Mrs. Ashmore turned away with a hasty *hope you feel better*.

Ashleigh left through the side door of the gym, hoping to call as little attention to herself as possible. No one appeared to notice her departure and she let out a relieved breath as she escaped outside into the cool spring air. She was walking back toward the front of the gym when she spotted Gina's car. She waited and watched as it crawled past the entrance then around to the side. As always, Gina seemed to know exactly where she was.

She pulled closer, then stopped. Gina got out and leaned across the top, her gaze raking over Ashleigh's body, sending chills down her spine.

"You look beautiful," Gina whispered. "Like a princess."

"Thank you."

"You would have done the prom queen proud. Sure you don't want to stay?"

Ashleigh shook her head. "I'd rather be with you."

Gina nodded and walked around the car, holding the door open for her. "Your chariot, my queen," she said with a bow.

Ashleigh laughed quietly as she got inside the old Toyota that Gina hated. As soon as they were out of the parking lot, Gina's hand found hers.

"You really do look lovely, Ashleigh. As beautiful as I've ever seen you."

Ashleigh squeezed her hand. "I wanted to look beautiful for you, not for them, not for James." She shivered when Gina brought her hand to her lips and kissed it, her tongue darting out for a brief touch, letting Ashleigh know what was to come. She shivered again as she imagined all that tongue would do to her.

Ashleigh's house was dark and quiet, as she expected. As soon as the door was closed, she was in Gina's arms, her mouth opening to her kiss.

"God, I love you," Gina whispered.

"I'll always love you." Ashleigh's hands found Gina's breasts, loving the way Gina moaned when she touched them. But she pulled away. "Let me leave my mom a note so she won't come into my room when they get home."

"Okay. Hurry."

Ashleigh did, scribbling out her lie before leading Gina upstairs to her bedroom. Once there, Gina turned on the lamp, her gaze again lingering on Ashleigh.

"May I have this dance?"

Ashleigh smiled. "You can have every dance."

There was no music except what they heard in their hearts— their souls—but they moved slowly together, their bodies pressing

125

close, their feet shuffling on the carpet without rhyme or reason as they had their prom dance. And as if on cue, Ashleigh lifted her head, finding Gina's mouth waiting. Their dance ended as their passion ignited and Ashleigh's beautiful prom dress was tossed on the floor as an afterthought, her only concern at the moment was Gina...and all she was about to do to her.

CHAPTER TWENTY-THREE

Present Day

Gina felt a bit self-conscious as she made her way to the ballroom. Most of the other women were dressed in near formal attire, none in slacks. But she reminded herself she was what she was, and she was who she was. And formal attire and Gina Granbury did not mix.

"Screw it," she murmured as she entered, no longer caring. She glanced around, instinctively knowing Ashleigh wasn't there yet. She found it amazing—and a little disconcerting—that she could still feel Ashleigh's presence, still find her in a crowded room. All this after twenty years.

She spotted Crissy and made her way over to her. While she and Crissy had never really been friends, only tolerating each other because of Ashleigh, she found Crissy's personality had grown on her. No longer the airheaded cheerleader, yet every bit as gregarious, she was the perfect hostess for the reunion. She smiled and waved Gina over.

"Gina, do you remember Sarah Reed?"

Gina smiled apologetically. "I'm sorry, no." She shook Sarah's hand. "It feels like I left here the day after graduation and just forgot everyone I'd ever known."

"That's okay. This is my first time back too. I joined the military," she explained.

"I see. Been around the world, huh?"

"A few times. Well, I should go find Mark. Good to see you again, Crissy."

Gina raised her eyebrows.

"Well, you didn't remember her. Should she have said 'nice to meet you'?" Crissy stood back and appraised her. "Wow. I never really could picture you in a gown, anyway."

"So you wouldn't be shocked if I told you I didn't own a dress?"

"Not in the least. You were always the jock. In fact, I used to think you were gay. It never occurred to me Ashleigh was."

Gina just smiled and shrugged.

"But wait." Crissy frowned. "You never married."

"A lot of people don't marry," Gina said easily. Then she tilted her head, feeling Ashleigh's presence in the room.

"Oh, my God," Crissy whispered.

Gina turned, following Crissy's gaze. *Oh, my God*, indeed. Ashleigh stood in the entryway, looking like a vision from heaven. Gina felt that old familiar tug at her heart when Ashleigh smiled at her. Gina stared, her eyes greedily traveling over Ashleigh's body, the tiny black strapless clinging deliciously to every curve... every curve that Gina once knew intimately.

She finally looked up, meeting Ashleigh's eyes. She couldn't believe the nervousness she felt as Ashleigh came toward her. It was like she was in high school all over again when Ashleigh's mere presence sent her into a tailspin. But she wasn't in high school and Ashleigh was no schoolgirl. She was a beautiful woman. A woman who still took her breath away.

"You look...stunning," Gina said softly.

"Thank you." Ashleigh moved closer. "You look quite

handsome yourself."

Gina felt a blush cross her face and was thankful for the muted lighting in the room.

"Ashleigh Pence, good grief, woman," Crissy said. "You now have all the married men drooling and the women thankful you're a lesbian."

Ashleigh laughed. "Thanks a lot, Crissy. I'm sure you meant that as a compliment."

"You look gorgeous in that dress." She leaned closer. "Are you *sure* you're gay?"

Ashleigh met Gina's gaze. "Very."

"Pity. I see James Simpson making his way over. Apparently, he's got that crush going again."

"He never could take a hint," Ashleigh said.

"Maybe it's the dress," Gina said, unable to stop herself from staring, her eyes glued to the plunging neckline, the swell of Ashleigh's breasts visible when she turned.

"Glad you like it," Ashleigh said as she caught Gina staring.

Gina blushed immediately. "Sorry. I...I'm—"

"Gosh, Ashleigh, you look fabulous," James said, saving Gina from further embarrassment.

"Thank you, James."

"I came by to claim a dance," he said. "The only opportunity we had was the prom, and you got sick. Remember?"

"I remember," Ashleigh said, chancing a glance Gina's way.

"So is that a yes?"

"Of course. Come find me," she said, albeit a bit awkwardly. When he finally moved away, Ashleigh turned to her. "I swear, it's like we're back in high school and he's got that look in his eyes again."

"Which look is that?"

"The *I'm-so-horny* teenager look. When I first talked with him, I got the feeling that he was gay, just closeted. But maybe not. Maybe—"

"Maybe he's carried a torch for you all these years?"

Ashleigh smiled. "Yeah, that would be crazy, wouldn't it."

129

"Very crazy."

Ashleigh moved closer. "Will you dance with me?"

"Determined to get tongues wagging, aren't you?"

"I don't care what any of these people say or think, Gina. They're not a part of my life."

"And they're certainly not a part of mine." Gina was surprised at how badly she wanted that dance. Ashleigh was dressed in next to nothing. To think she'd be in Gina's arms again after all these years made Gina's heart race just a bit faster. "Of all the scenarios I played out at the prospect of seeing you again, dancing was not one of them."

Ashleigh laughed. "God, mine either. I envisioned meeting you with a curt nod and then not speaking to you the entire time."

The DJ Crissy had hired was all set up and music started. She'd promised he'd do a mix of current favorites and oldies from when they were in high school. She didn't, however, warn of the reenactment of the prom dance.

"Hello everyone," Crissy greeted from the microphone. "Let me first say how grateful I am for the large turnout." She stepped away, leading the applause. "I see so many new faces here, those who didn't make the ten-year reunion. Thank you for coming," she said, her glance landing on Gina. "Before we get started on a fun evening of dancing and partying, let me remind you of the brunch scheduled for tomorrow morning, for those of you who don't have to leave early. Now, as a special treat, let's go back to our senior prom. Some of you may remember that Ashleigh Pence was voted prom queen, but got sick the night of the prom."

"Oh my God," Ashleigh whispered. "I'll kill her."

"I had to settle for runner-up," Crissy said, "and was forced to dance with Brian." She rolled her eyes dramatically, drawing laughter. "Well, I think Ashleigh needs her due. How about a prom dance?"

The music started and Ashleigh nearly clung to Gina as Brian made his way over. He bowed gallantly, holding out his hand. Ashleigh took it, glancing quickly at Gina before going out to the dance floor.

Crissy joined Gina on the sidelines, her smile contagious. "Oh, I so owed her for that," she said as she held up her camera and snapped a picture.

"Ashleigh hated the whole prom thing," Gina said.

"I know. She hated the whole cheerleader thing too." Crissy clapped as Brian spun Ashleigh around, her black dress flowing out, exposing tan, lean thighs.

Gina's breath caught at the sight. After twenty years, she still felt that desire she always had for Ashleigh.

"My God, that dress is a killer," Crissy said. "Is she beautiful or what?"

"Gorgeous," Gina said.

The dance finally came to an end and relief washed over Ashleigh's face as she and Brian came over to them, the applause dying down as another song started, prompting the others onto the dance floor.

"You know I'm going to have to kill you for that, right?"

Crissy laughed. "I owed you." She linked her arm through Brian's. "And now I'm going to dance with my husband." She glanced behind Ashleigh. "Word of warning. James is coming over."

Ashleigh's eyes found Gina's and she moved closer, again causing Gina's pulse to race. "I so wish he'd leave me alone."

"Tell him."

"Tell him what? He knows I'm gay." She stepped away from Gina as James approached.

"Ashleigh, may I have this dance?"

Gina saw the smile Ashleigh forced to her face.

"Of course, James."

Gina felt a tiny stab of jealously as she watched Ashleigh move into James's arms. She recognized it as the same jealously she felt in high school when Ashleigh's mother talked her into accepting a date with James. There was nothing she could do about it then and nothing she could do about it now.

She turned away from the dance floor and went to the bar.

As many times as Ashleigh had mentioned them dancing, she didn't really think they would. Despite Ashleigh's assertion that she didn't care what anyone thought, it was still Calloway, a small, conservative south Texas town. Would they really go on the dance floor together—two supposedly best friends from high school? They'd kept their secret then, but surely everyone would put two and two together. Ashleigh's broken heart in college before coming out, Gina's "never married" status, the two of them inseparable in high school, both without boyfriends.

And really, was there a reason for them to dance? Ashleigh was involved with someone. She was in a relationship. The fact that they'd somewhat repaired their friendship was one thing. Completely different to fall into old habits and flirt with the attraction they both still had. Yes, Ashleigh felt it too, she could see that. And the dress? Good Lord, it was enough to send her over the edge, as Ashleigh must have known it would. So what would a dance possibly do? What would she do if Ashleigh slipped into her arms? Would she hold her at an appropriately proper distance away, as a friend would? Or would she be tempted to pull her close, to feel Ashleigh's body against her own, even if for only one last time?

She knew the answer would be the latter.

Gina downed her drink, thankful the reunion was coming to a close. She needed to put some space between them. The last thing she needed was to go back to Corpus, her head and heart full of Ashleigh Pence again. Perhaps she was right to have dreaded the reunion, although for completely different reasons.

"You hiding?"

She turned to find Crissy standing beside her, a questioning look in her eyes.

She held up her empty glass. "Just a quick drink."

Crissy leaned on the bar beside her. "Forgive me for speculating, but I was watching you when Ashleigh went to dance with James. Well, at first, I was watching Ashleigh and she had that same look she used to get in high school whenever we went out and James thought it was a date. Then I looked at you. And it finally hit me."

Gina turned to her, not knowing what to say. She raised her eyebrows.

"You and Ashleigh were already seeing each other in high school. You're the one she called whenever she needed to escape from James. So I'm guessing you're the one who broke her heart in college. That's why, after being best friends in high school, you've had no contact all these years." Crissy bumped her shoulder. "Am I right?"

"It's a little more complicated than that, but yes, you're right."

Crissy grinned broadly. "I knew it. And now here you meet up again, you're both single. You are really single, right?"

"I am, yes. Ashleigh's not."

"Of course she is. She's always been single."

Gina shook her head. "No. She's in a relationship. Has been for several years."

"*Ashleigh?* No, she's not."

"Yes. With Faith."

"Who? Look, I saw her at Christmas and she was dreading coming to the reunion and still being single. In fact, she said I should shoot her and put her out of her misery if she turns forty and is still single."

Gina frowned. "But—" Could it be true? Was that why the mention of Faith was such a shock to Ashleigh's mother? "Why would she tell me she's in a relationship then?"

"I don't know. Maybe she—"

"Hey, you two."

They both turned as Ashleigh walked over to them. Gina's mind was still racing and she couldn't meet Ashleigh's eyes.

"He insisted on two dances. I think that was my quota for him," Ashleigh said. "What are you two doing?"

"Just visiting," Crissy said. "Catching up." She moved away. "I should find my husband though. Talk to you later."

Ashleigh turned to Gina. "She's acting weird."

"Is she?"

133

"So are you."

Gina smiled. "She figured it out."

"What out?"

"About high school. Us."

"She did?" Ashleigh stood against the bar and raised her hand to the bartender. "Well, I'm surprised it took her this long." She looked at Gina. "You want another?"

"Yes, please."

"Hi. Me again," she said to the bartender.

"The good stuff?"

"Yes. Gina, what are you having?"

"Bourbon."

Ashleigh smiled at the bartender. "Two of the good stuff, please." When he went to make their drinks, Ashleigh said, "I tipped him twenty bucks last night. I'm glad he remembered."

"A twenty-buck tip in Calloway? How could he forget?"

"Here you go, ladies."

"Thanks." Ashleigh again shoved a twenty at him. "Keep the change."

"Enjoy your drinks."

They sipped their drinks quietly, standing close, saying nothing. Gina could feel the electricity between them. She wondered if Ashleigh felt it too.

"I still want that dance," Ashleigh said quietly.

Gina nodded. *Yes, she feels it.*

"Unless, since Crissy figured it out, you're afraid others will as well."

"Doesn't matter to me," Gina said truthfully. "I don't plan on returning to Calloway anytime soon. And you know, these people, they were never really friends."

"No. You weren't close with anyone, were you?"

Gina shook her head. "Coming in late, in the ninth grade, everyone had already established friendships. Besides, I had a secret then. I didn't want anyone to find out."

Ashleigh smiled and moved closer. "I never told you this before, but I used to feel you watching me. Sometimes I would catch you watching me. It wasn't something I was afraid of. I think, on another level, I knew what it was. And when we finally got a chance to be around each other—"

"At Jennifer's swim party."

"Yes." Ashleigh laughed. "They were trying to set you up with Brian. He thought you were hot."

Gina turned to face her. "I thought *you* were hot." She was surprised at the quick blush that lit up Ashleigh's face.

"I never, ever, felt any kind of a spark with someone," Ashleigh said. "Until that day. I got out of the pool in my bikini and you were watching me. The look in your eyes...well, it gave me chills. I knew then I was attracted to you."

Gina stared at her, meeting her gaze without flinching. "Why are we talking about this?"

"I'm not sure. Maybe just trying to make sense of it all."

Sense of their attraction? Or sense of their breakup? Gina decided it didn't matter. They'd spent twenty years apart. But that old attraction was still there. What sense did that make? And what about Faith? Did she exist or not? Again, right now, it didn't matter.

"Dance with me," Gina said, her voice quiet. She couldn't place the song and had no idea if it was a current favorite or an oldie, but it was slow enough for them to dance. The look in Ashleigh's eyes took her breath away.

"I'd love to."

Gina ignored the curious stares of the others, blocking out everyone but Ashleigh. When she pulled her close, she felt a slight tremor in Ashleigh's body.

"Nervous? Or embarrassed?"

Ashleigh smiled. "I was never embarrassed to be with you, Gina. I'm certainly not about to start now."

It was Gina's turn to tremble as Ashleigh's arms circled her neck. Gina gave in, pulling Ashleigh against her, letting in memories from so long ago. Their feet shuffled aimlessly as they moved and Gina felt Ashleigh's rapid heartbeat against her breasts. She closed her eyes, pretending, just for a second, that this was how it would have been, had they stayed together.

"You do realize we're the best looking couple out here," Ashleigh said as she whispered into her ear.

"Must be the dress." Gina pulled back slightly, seeing the flirty look in Ashleigh's eyes. Ah, so she wanted to play. No harm in flirting when there was a roomful of people to keep them in line. "You always did like to go braless," she said, her eyes lowering to the swell of breast that was exposed. "It used to drive me crazy."

Ashleigh arched an eyebrow. "Used to?"

Gina pulled her tight, their breasts smashing together. "Still does," she whispered, surprised at how daring she had become. She nearly stumbled as Ashleigh moaned into her ear.

"We should stop," Ashleigh said.

"You started it."

"I never could control myself in your arms."

Gina turned them around slowly, her hands keeping Ashleigh pressed close. "Did you wear the dress for me?"

"Yes."

"Why?"

The song ended and Ashleigh pulled away, her grin wicked. "Why would you think?" She tugged Gina's hand, leading her off the floor and toward the table where Crissy and Brian sat.

"Oh, God, you are so busted," Crissy said.

"What do you mean?"

She held out her camera, showing it to them. Gina's breath caught, seeing the two of them in each other's arms, their bodies molded together. There was no doubt they'd been lovers. Their bodies were too familiar with each other.

Ashleigh turned, meeting Gina's gaze. "Maybe dancing wasn't such a good idea."

Ashleigh made her way back from the ladies' room having to stop no less than four times to say, yes, she and Gina had been an item way back when. All that from one dance. Yet a dance she would never forget. God, how wonderful had it been to be in Gina's arms again? But how crazy was it? How could she still be attracted to her after all these years? How could she have dreaded the reunion, dreaded seeing Gina again then end up flirting with her—shamelessly.

And why was Gina flirting back? Surely they both knew how dangerous it was. There was a time when only a look between them would send them into each other's arms, into bed, making love. It only took a look. No words needed to be spoken. Then why did she think it would be different now? Because they were twenty years older? Because she'd made up a phantom lover in Faith? Did she think she could flirt with Gina and nothing would happen because there was Faith?

What have I done?

Indeed. She was now embarrassed for the way she'd acted, the way she'd flirted. What must Gina think of her? Here she supposedly had a lover, yet she was flirting with another woman. Did Gina doubt her now? Did she think that perhaps yes, Ashleigh had been cheating on her in college?

She let out a heavy sigh, then avoided the others, making her way to the bar instead. She obviously couldn't be trusted to act like an adult in Gina's presence.

She smiled quickly at the bartender. "Make it a double. High school reunions are brutal."

"So they say."

She turned her back to him, not wanting to make small talk. He seemed to get the hint as he left her drink on the bar and walked away.

She spent the next few hours nursing two drinks, avoiding Gina, avoiding Crissy but dancing with Brian, and finally dancing with James again and admitting to him that yes, she and Gina had been lovers in high school and that's the real reason she wouldn't date him. He said he always suspected there was something between her and Gina but still didn't believe it, even when word got out that Ashleigh was gay.

It was a crazy way to end the reunion, she knew. But thankfully, end it did. And tomorrow, they would all go their separate ways. She'd already decided she'd skip the brunch. She would head over to her mother's and spend the day by the pool. Gina would head back to Corpus and that would be that.

She turned, feeling Gina watching her. For all the avoiding she'd done, Gina hadn't been exactly searching her out. But she walked toward her now, her eyes intense as they peered at her.

"Share an elevator?"

Ashleigh nodded. It would be rude to refuse the offer. She walked beside Gina, the effects of her double bourbons catching up with her. She leaned against the wall, waiting for the elevator.

"You did an effective job of avoiding me," Gina said.

"Yes."

"Something I did?"

Ashleigh shook her head. "Not you. Me."

The doors opened and Ashleigh went inside, again leaning against the wall, watching Gina. Gina looked at her questioningly.

"Third floor," Ashleigh said.

Gina pushed both buttons for the second and third floors. "I'm on two," she explained.

"Are you heading back to Corpus early?" Ashleigh asked.

Gina shook her head. "Actually, I'm staying in town for the week. I promised Aunt Lou I'd spend some time with her."

Ashleigh sighed. "Imagine that."

"Why? What time are you leaving?"

"I'm staying for a few days too. Courtney is coming down from San Antonio Monday. We're going to catch up."

Gina took a step toward her and Ashleigh braced herself against the wall. The bell chimed, signaling the stop on the second floor.

"Maybe we'll run into each other then," Gina said, her voice quiet.

Ashleigh nodded, unable to take her gaze away from Gina.

"Goodnight," Gina said. She turned to go, then paused, looking back at Ashleigh, her eyes lowering to Ashleigh's lips. Unconsciously, Ashleigh wetted them, waiting. She was breathing fast, she knew, as Gina lowered her head. To her embarrassment, she moaned even before Gina's lips touched hers. The kiss was very light, but enough to conjure up delicious memories and leave Ashleigh wanting more. Her eyes must have said as much because Gina's mouth found hers again, this time harder, their quiet moans echoing together in the empty elevator. Ashleigh's hands gripped Gina's waist, holding her close as the kiss deepened. She felt her legs grow weak as Gina's tongue brushed against her lower lip before pulling away.

Then she was gone, slipping away before Ashleigh could make a total fool of herself and beg Gina for more. Beg her for much, much more. The doors slid closed, leaving Ashleigh leaning against the wall, her fingers touching her lips where only seconds before, Gina's mouth had been.

CHAPTER TWENTY-FOUR

Present Day

Ashleigh splashed water on her heated skin as she lazily floated in her parents' pool. Her father, while at retirement age, couldn't seem to give up his job at Foster's Natural Gas, saying the place would fall apart without him. Actually, he was one of those people who *had* to have a job in order to feel productive. That, and driving around the area inspecting natural gas wells gave him the freedom he still needed. She suspected he would go crazy—and take her mother with him—if he was stuck in the house all day.

Her mother was off to the grocery store to stock up for Courtney's visit. Her mother loved to cook and no doubt they would have all of their childhood favorites while they were here.

So, alone, Ashleigh donned her bikini and got in the pool, swimming laps before pulling one of the floats into the water. She had done a remarkable job of keeping Gina Granbury out of her mind. Yesterday, Sunday, she'd shared both lunch and dinner with her parents, talking for hours as they caught up. She'd slept soundly, the quiet of Calloway lulling her into a blissful sleep. Now, today, with no distractions, she found her thoughts going to her former lover. Wonder what the odds were that they would both stay over in Calloway after the reunion? She'd suspected Gina would be on the road back home as soon as it was over. But no. She was here the week. *Maybe we'll run into each other.* And maybe they wouldn't. Because if the scene in the elevator didn't tell them they still had an attraction between them, nothing would. She had been ready to shed her clothes right then and there and make love.

Make love?

She closed her eyes, letting the gentle rocking motion of the water take her back twenty years, seeing them, not as adults, but as teenagers. There had been nothing awkward about them being lovers. The most awkward thing was finding time to be alone—and not getting caught. But their lovemaking? No, it had none of the clumsiness—or ineptness—that comes with being teenagers. They always had a connection between them, a sixth sense that guided them. Even the first time, the first time for either of them, they just *knew.*

She opened her eyes, looking across the water, seeing Gina splashing in the pool, her long dark hair slicked back. She remembered the torture she endured, Gina walking around shamelessly in her tiny bikini, teasing and flirting, and Ashleigh could do nothing about it as her mother or siblings would undoubtedly be about. All Ashleigh could do was stare—and wait. Wait for nighttime, when they could be alone in her room. She got her revenge then, her mouth and tongue teasing Gina mercilessly, making her beg for the release she sought. Even then, as teens, they were playing adult games.

What would it be like now? What if Ashleigh hadn't invented Faith? They would both be single. The old attraction was obviously still there. That was evident from the dance, from the kiss in the elevator, from the looks between them. Both single, was there then any reason they shouldn't explore the adult attraction

141

they had?

No.

She flipped off the float and into the water, sinking below the surface. No, the only thing stopping them was Faith, her imaginary girlfriend. In the elevator, she could tell by the hesitation in Gina that she was considering the fact that Ashleigh was involved with someone. But still, they couldn't resist a kiss.

Gina paced aimlessly in Aunt Lou's living room, waiting while her aunt dressed for lunch. Gina was taking her to one of the new restaurants that had opened on the north side of town. It was Tuesday and she'd decided that she had been over-ambitious when she said she would stay the week in Calloway. She realized that she and Aunt Lou communicated much better over the phone than in person. And why wouldn't they? That had been their relationship since she'd left Calloway twenty years ago, except for a handful of times, the last being her father's funeral. After two days, the effort—for both of them—to keep each other entertained had reached new heights when Gina had suggested lunch out, anything to get them away from the house. Thankfully, she'd kept the hotel room for the week and not accepted Aunt Lou's invitation to bunk with her.

It didn't help that she couldn't get her mind off of Ashleigh, either. Ashleigh and the kiss. She knew she owed Ashleigh an apology for that. How arrogant of her to assume Ashleigh wanted her kiss in the first place. But the dance, the intimacy of it all, begged for them to kiss. Whether Ashleigh was involved with someone or not—and according to Crissy, she was not—that didn't matter. Ashleigh *told* her she was in a relationship. That should have been enough to deter any thoughts of kissing. And it nearly was. But in the end, Gina couldn't resist. The pull was too strong. In all fairness, it wasn't she who prolonged the kiss, it wasn't she who gripped Ashleigh's waist, holding her in place.

No, Ashleigh turned her brief kiss into more. Ashleigh was the one who held tight to Gina when she tried to pull away. All of which only confused her more. Instinct told her to get the hell out of Calloway...and fast. Leave. Go back to Corpus, back to her life. There were too many memories here, too many luscious memories of the two of them. She closed her eyes, remembering the countless times they'd touched, kissed and pleasured each other. Two teenagers in love, sneaking off any chance they got, hiding in shadows, stealing kisses, throwing caution aside as they made love, unable to stop, unable to wait even a second longer.

"It was incredible," she murmured quietly. Yes, it had been. Twenty years ago. And no one had touched her that way since. It was rather distressing to realize that probably no one would ever touch her like that again.

"Sorry that took so long. I couldn't decide what to wear."

Gina pushed her thoughts away, turning with a smile to Aunt Lou, seeing her in a pretty summer dress. "A dress?" She pointed at her own shorts and sandals. "Too casual?"

"Oh, don't be silly. I just haven't had a lunch date before. In case someone from church sees me, I wanted to be dressed appropriately."

Gina bit her tongue, knowing her words would fall on deaf ears. This was Aunt Lou's town, these were her people. If she wanted to put on airs and play a part, that was her business.

CHAPTER TWENTY-FIVE

Present Day

"This is heaven," Courtney said as she lazily drifted on her float in their parents' pool.

"And judging by your pasty skin, you don't get to experience it much."

"And judging by your obnoxiously tan skin, you don't work for a living."

Ashleigh laughed. "I work plenty. I just choose to spend my free time outdoors."

"And I prefer to spend my free time indoors with my husband," Courtney shot back. "Something you would know nothing about."

Ashleigh splashed water on her. "You spend your free time with your nose stuck in a book. Your husband would be the first to tell us that."

Courtney returned her splash. "So, what's with your love life?"

"What love life?"

"Mom says you're seeing someone. Faith."

"Oh *God*," Ashleigh groaned. "She told you?"

"Of course. You dating anyone is big news."

Ashleigh debated telling her the truth, deciding it would do no good to keep pretending Faith existed.

"You're going to think I'm crazy."

"Probably, yes."

"You remember Gina Granbury?"

"I should. She spent nearly every weekend here with us."

Ashleigh leaned her head back into the water. "Oh, great," she muttered.

"Great what?"

Ashleigh stared at her. If she told about why she made up Faith, she'd be confessing to her affair with Gina during high school. That was something she wasn't sure she wanted Courtney or her mother to know.

"What?" Courtney asked again.

"Look, promise me what I'm about to tell you, you will *never* tell Mom."

"Ashleigh, you're nearly forty. Is it necessary to still keep secrets from Mom?"

"Telling someone they're nearly forty is not a compliment. You know that, right?"

"Will you just tell me already."

Ashleigh sighed. "Well, it's the reunion. And the fact that Gina was coming."

"What about the reunion?"

"I assumed Gina would be involved with someone, be in a relationship, and I didn't want to be single. So I made up Faith."

Courtney stared at her, eyebrows raised. "You made up a girlfriend? Because of Gina?"

"Yes."

"You made up a girlfriend and you told *Mom* about her? Yeah, you're crazy."

"I only had to tell Mom because Gina came over to the house."

"And what does Gina having a boyfriend have to do with you needing a girlfriend?"

Ashleigh rolled her eyes. "I swear, for someone as smart as you are, you are clueless."

"I'm pretty sure that wasn't a compliment."

"Gina wouldn't have a *boyfriend*, Courtney."

"She's married then?"

"No, she's not married." Ashleigh waited, still seeing a blank look in Courtney's eyes. "Hello? She's gay."

"Gina?"

"Yes, Gina."

Finally, a glimmer of light, then her eyes widened. "Gina's gay? Then...oh my God," she whispered. "You and Gina?"

Ashleigh nodded. "Yes."

"Oh my God!" she shrieked. "Are you serious?"

Ashleigh glanced quickly to the house, hoping her mother wouldn't come to investigate Courtney's antics. "Keep your voice down."

"In high school?"

"Yes, in high school."

"All those times she—"

"Yes."

"Oh my God. I cannot believe it." She tipped over her float and swam to Ashleigh's, holding on to the side. "That's so cool."

"You're a doctor. You're old. You can't say *that's so cool*. It's just wrong."

"I should have known. I think I did know, I just didn't put two and two together."

"You did not know."

Courtney grinned. "Remember how Mark had such a huge crush on her. When she'd come over to swim, he used to just stare at her."

"Yeah, Mark, the big queen, had a crush on my girlfriend."

Courtney laughed. "But that's how I should have known. You used to stare at her too."

"I did not."

146

"Yes, you did. You couldn't keep your eyes off her. I used to think it was envy of her body or something. I didn't know you were like, really looking at her with lust or anything."

"It wasn't lust." Ashleigh turned serious. "Well, not just lust. It was love."

"She's the one who broke your heart in college."

"Yes."

Courtney led them into shallow water where she could stand. "How did you ever pull that off without Mom and Dad finding out?"

"I have no idea."

"When did it start?"

"Down at the coast. The summer before our junior year."

"I remember. Crissy always went with us, but that year you invited Gina."

"Yes. I had no idea I was gay, but I knew that I was attracted to her. I just wasn't sure what it all meant."

"Gina?"

"Gina knew she was gay."

"She didn't force you or anything, did she?"

"Good Lord, no. If anything, I started it," Ashleigh said. She raised her hand. "But I don't want to talk about all that. The thing is, we haven't spoken in twenty years. I have secretly hated her for twenty years. So when I found out she was coming to the reunion, I panicked. Here I was, still single."

"So you made up a lover?"

"Yeah."

"That is so childish."

"Whatever."

"Okay, so now Mom thinks you have a girlfriend. Just break up with her when you get home, call Mom, and all will be back to normal."

"Gina also thinks I have a girlfriend."

"Yeah, I thought that was your plan all along, wasn't it."

Ashleigh splashed water at Courtney again. "Yes, that was the plan. The problem is, Gina is single."

"So? So you one-upped her. She's still single and you've got a girlfriend. What's the big deal?"

"God, I swear, you are clueless."

"Well, if you would quit talking in circles, perhaps I could follow you."

"I dreaded seeing her again. It turns out she was dreading it as well. But we talked. We cleared the air about some things. There were some communication issues in college and some misunderstandings. So we talked."

"Good. You were best friends."

"We were best friends and lovers. And Gina is single. And I'm technically single. And the attraction is still there."

"After twenty years? Come on."

"I'm serious."

"Just because you talked, doesn't mean you could rekindle anything."

"Well, there was the dance. It was incredible."

"You *danced*? Oh my God. So you think Mom won't hear about that? It'll probably make the paper. *Two Women Seen Dancing in Hotel Ballroom*," she teased.

Ashleigh met her eyes. "And then the kiss in the elevator."

"You kissed in the elevator? Ashleigh, you do realize you're in Calloway, not Houston." She leaned closer. "You *kissed*?"

"Yes." Ashleigh grabbed her hand. "I nearly melted right there. And I wanted more than a kiss, Courtney. I think she did too."

"Well then?"

"Duh. There's Faith."

"Oh my God. Your fantasy lover is keeping you from—"

"I know it's silly," Ashleigh said. "But the fact is, Gina thinks there's a Faith, and so she won't pursue anything. I know her."

"So tell her the truth."

"No. She'll think I'm a pathetic, lonely old woman."

"She may just think you're insane, which is the direction I'm leaning."

Ashleigh sighed. "Or I could just do nothing. I'm leaving

tomorrow. I doubt I'll ever see her again."

"Wait a minute. Gina's still here? In Calloway?"

"Yes. She's staying the week so she and her aunt can catch up."

"Why didn't you say something?"

"What for?"

"That's why you haven't wanted to leave the house. That's why we've been in this pool for two days. You're afraid you'll run into her."

"Yes."

"Well, that's just crazy."

"You keep using that word. You're starting to make me consider it."

"Let's invite her for dinner tonight."

"No! Now who's talking crazy?"

"Come on. It'll be fun. Dad's doing steaks. We'll be out here. It'll be very casual."

Ashleigh shook her head. "I don't think that's a very good idea."

CHAPTER TWENTY-SIX

Present Day

"Of all the invitations I thought I might get this week, getting a call from Ashleigh's baby sister wasn't one of them." Gina patted the leather seat. "And a chauffeured ride at that."

"I wanted a chance to talk to you."

"I take it Ashleigh doesn't know I'm coming to dinner."

"Well, she won't be totally surprised. It went like this. Me, *let's invite Gina to dinner*. Her, *I don't think that's a very good idea*."

Gina laughed. "She's afraid to see me."

"You could say that."

"I take it you know."

"Oh yeah. She spilled her guts." Courtney reached across the console and playfully tapped her leg. "And I can't believe Mom and Dad never caught you."

Gina looked at her thoughtfully. "Why is Ashleigh afraid to see me?"

"Why do you think?"

"The kiss in the elevator."

"That. And the dance."

"The dance was innocent."

"Whatever."

"Whatever?"

"Look, my sister's been single forever. So when she starts talking about attraction and melting from your kiss and all that crap, well, I couldn't stand on the sidelines and let her make a complete fool out of herself."

"Courtney, she's not single, so don't try to play matchmaker."

"You mean Faith?"

"Yes. And I may have done a lot of things when I was younger, but now, no way would I come between two people who are in a relationship. I just don't do that."

"Okay, just between you and me, my sister's an idiot."

Gina laughed. "What's she done?"

"I can't tell you. She'll never speak to me again. But if you can get into that tiny brain of hers, maybe you can figure it out." Courtney pulled into her parents' driveway and stopped. "Of course, when she sees you, she may not be speaking to me anyway."

"But your mom knows I'm coming right? I'm not just crashing dinner?"

"She knows. Ashleigh thinks I went to pick up some rolls or something." Courtney opened her door and Gina did the same. "By the way, I left her out by the pool, if you're interested."

Gina grinned. "Bikini?"

"Tiny black one, yeah."

"Okay. Let me at least say hello to your mother first."

And she did, sticking her head into the kitchen as Mrs. Pence was stabbing a fork into several large potatoes. Mrs. Pence winked at her and waved her out to the patio. Apparently the whole family was playing matchmaker.

She walked outside, finding Ashleigh immediately. She'd just pulled herself out of the water, her back to Gina. Gina stared, taking in every inch of exposed skin, glistening wet as the last rays of the evening sun touched her. She remained quiet, watching as

Ashleigh reached for a towel, tousling her hair before dabbing at her body. Then Ashleigh's shoulders stiffened and Gina knew she'd felt her presence. Ashleigh turned slowly, using the towel to cover herself.

"I'll kill her," she said.

Gina walked closer. "It's getting a little bloody around here, isn't it? First Crissy, now your sister."

Ashleigh nodded but didn't say anything else. Gina couldn't tell if she was angry that Courtney had invited her for dinner or still upset by the kiss they'd shared in the elevator. Gina assumed the kiss.

"Look, I should apologize," Gina started, waiting for Ashleigh's response.

"For?" she asked vaguely.

"I had no right to kiss you. I'm sorry. I know you're in a relationship and I didn't mean to belittle that by kissing you."

Ashleigh looked away, feigning sudden interest in her towel. "Why did you kiss me?' she finally asked.

"I don't know. I guess it's just being back here...all the memories, all that stuff. I realize we're not in high school anymore, Ashleigh. We're two completely different people than we were back then. I'm sorry. I crossed the line."

Ashleigh gave her a slight smile. "Yeah. Just memories and all. And you know, that dance didn't help."

"Your idea."

"True."

"So? We're friends? You're not mad?"

Ashleigh took a deep breath, watching Gina as she exhaled. She nodded. "Friends."

"Good." Gina stepped closer, arching her eyebrows teasingly. "It would help immensely if you'd put some clothes on though."

Ashleigh sipped her wine as she watched Gina being grilled by her father. Well, perhaps *grilled* was too harsh a word. Her father had always been straightforward and to the point, no need throwing pretty adjectives in to gloss over things.

"Is it just me or does Dad seem extremely interested in what Gina's been doing the last twenty years?" Courtney asked.

"I blame the whole evening on you," Ashleigh said, straining to hear what her father and Gina were discussing.

"It was fun, you have to admit. I had forgotten how charming Gina was."

Yeah, she was charming. And just like in high school, Gina could flirt with her in such a subtle way that no one knew. At least, Ashleigh didn't think anyone knew. She, however, was attuned to each and every glance and comment. The fact that Gina was flirting with her in the first place didn't disturb her as much as her reaction to it. She'd never been able to resist Gina. Never. Now—like back then—she found her body responding to Gina. She recognized the pull, the attraction. It was no different than it had been when they were young. Each glance drew her nearer, each innocent touch made her crave more. Even now, she couldn't take her eyes off Gina. She blatantly stared, taking advantage as her father distracted Gina. She followed the length of her bare legs, as long and muscular as she remembered—runner's legs. The body she looked at now wasn't the rail thin image of a teen, however. It was the full, mature body of an adult woman, curves and softness blending with the firmness that comes with regular exercise. As her glance settled on Gina's breasts, a vivid picture suddenly popped in her mind and she drew a sharp breath, her mind's eye reflecting an image of her mouth settling over Gina's hard nipple, her tongue teasing her until Gina was begging for release.

"You okay?"

Ashleigh felt the hot blush on her face and she reached for her glass, the wine nearly spilling as she hastily drank. She took a deep breath. "I'm fine."

"You don't look fine." Courtney leaned closer. "I think you should tell her."

"Tell her what?"

"Now who's clueless?"

"Look, I'm leaving tomorrow. Going back to Houston.

153

Everything will be back to normal."

"Yes. You're going back to your empty condo, your loveless life. Going back to the job you hate in a city you hate."

"All of which has nothing to do with Gina Granbury."

"Tell her you're still attracted to her."

"I will not."

"Why?"

"Because. It's far too late. We're too old. Too much time has passed."

"Those are silly excuses. What are you afraid of?"

"I'm afraid—" But she stopped, closing her mouth as Gina finally escaped her father and came back to the table to join them. "Sorry," Ashleigh apologized. "He gets carried away sometimes."

"Oh, it's okay. I always liked your dad. Besides, he gave me some tips on grilling the perfect steak."

"I'm sure he did." Courtney laughed. "Did he share his secret rub?"

"As a matter of fact, he did."

"Wow. You must have really charmed him," Ashleigh said. "I don't think he's ever told anyone his recipe."

"I'm sworn to secrecy, so you won't get it out of me."

"More wine?" Courtney asked.

Gina shook her head. "No. I should probably head back to the hotel. Thanks for inviting me for dinner." She glanced at Ashleigh. "I hope me being here wasn't too awkward."

"No, not at all. I enjoyed it."

"Me too." Gina looked at them both, then raised her eyebrows. "I kinda need a ride."

"Oh, I completely forgot," Courtney said. "Ashleigh volunteered to take you back."

Ashleigh glared at her sister, a rebuttal on her lips. However, she knew it would do no good to protest. Courtney was smiling triumphantly as she sipped from her wine.

"Yes. I'll run you back," she said as she shoved away from the table, finding some solace in the situation as she pinched her sister on her arm as she walked past. She grinned at the muted *ouch* she heard.

"Good to see you again, Courtney."

Courtney stood and gave Gina a quick hug. "You too. It was nice to visit with you. If you're ever in San Antonio, look me up."

"Will do."

Ashleigh waited patiently as the scene was repeated with her parents. She was a little surprised by the affectionate hugs both her mother and father gave Gina, as well as the invitation to stop by if she was ever back in Calloway.

"You have a great family," Gina said as they backed out of the driveway.

"Thanks. They have their moments."

"You mean like Courtney volunteering you for the ride?"

"Yeah, that." Ashleigh smiled. "And dinner."

"Well, I enjoyed the evening. I'm glad she invited me."

Without thinking, Ashleigh reached over and squeezed Gina's arm. "I didn't mean that I didn't enjoy your company. I did."

Gina nodded. "So, you're leaving tomorrow?"

"Yes. I need to get back."

"I'm sure you miss...Faith and everything."

Ashleigh frowned at the slight hesitation. Was Gina starting to question whether Faith really existed or not? She tightened her grip on the steering wheel. Or—*and I'll kill her if she did*—had Courtney opened her big mouth and told Gina the truth?

She squared her shoulders. "Yes. I miss...her." She finally relaxed as the hotel came into view. The evening was nearly over.

"I'm really glad I came to the reunion, Ashleigh. It was good to see you again."

Ashleigh slowed, turning into one of the empty parking spots. She debated leaving the engine running, but thought that would be rude. "Yes. After dreading it as much as I was, I'm glad we had a chance to catch up."

Gina was quiet, then her glance slid to the hotel. "You want

155

to come up to the room?"

Ashleigh shook her head. "No, I...I should get going."

Gina tilted her head. "We'll probably never see each other again. You want to say goodbye in a car?"

"We used to do a lot of things in a car," Ashleigh blurted out, immediately wishing she could take the words back.

"Yes, we did. And I guess we said our share of goodbyes there."

Ashleigh looked at her, hearing just a hint of disappointment in her voice. Knowing she had no business going to Gina's hotel room, she gave in. "But you're right. We probably won't see each other again. I guess a proper goodbye is in order."

"Thank you."

They were silent as they walked into the hotel and down the short hallway to the elevators. The door opened immediately and they got in, Ashleigh leaning against the wall, mimicking her position from the other night. When she realized it, she pushed off the wall, turning away from Gina to stare at the doors. It was a short ride to the second floor and Gina motioned her off, then led the way to her room.

Ashleigh was actually nervous as Gina slid her key card into the slot, watching the green light flash before Gina pushed it open. Ashleigh followed her inside, hearing the distinct click as the door swung shut and locked.

"I'd offer you something to drink, but I never really stocked the fridge," Gina said.

"I'm okay. Thanks."

They stood several feet apart, watching each other. Ashleigh was afraid to go to her, afraid to hug her, afraid to say goodbye. As they'd said, they probably wouldn't see each other again. There was no reason to.

"Well, again, it was good to see you," Gina said, taking a step closer. She smiled slightly. "You've grown into a lovely woman, Ashleigh. But I think my memories of you will always be that of the beautiful teenager I fell in love with."

Ashleigh nodded as those words hit home, making her take

a step nearer to their goodbye. "Yes. When I think of you, I see the skinny girl with the long dark hair." She slowly reached out, touching Gina's hair. "But I like your hair shorter like this. It suits you," she said as her fingers threaded through the longer strands at her neck. She dared to meet Gina's eyes, surprised by the questions she saw. She immediately lowered her hand.

They were silent as seconds passed, then Gina spread her arms. Ashleigh moved to her without hesitation, her own arms circling Gina's shoulders as they both pulled each other closer. The hug started innocently enough, yet neither pulled away. Ashleigh closed her eyes, relishing the feel of Gina's body for what she knew would be the last time. Her arms tightened, as did Gina's, both of them moving closer still until their bodies were flush with each other, head to toe. Ashleigh bit her lip, trying so hard to feel nothing, willing her body to remain under her control and not Gina's. But—as had always been the case—her body didn't listen to her, not where Gina was concerned.

All it took was Gina's hands slipping lower, the light pressure there causing Ashleigh's hips to move, however slight. She moaned, feeling her body betray her as it simply melted in Gina's arms. It was she—not Gina—who pulled back, just enough to lift her head, just enough to find Gina's mouth. She gave up trying to pretend it was a goodbye hug as soon as their lips met. Memories crashed around her as their mouths opened to each other, tongues brushing together for the first time in twenty years.

She let herself go, her fingers tangling in Gina's hair, holding her close, their moans turning to groans as their kisses deepened. She felt Gina's hands cup her buttocks, squeezing hard, pulling Ashleigh's hips intimately against her.

Ashleigh pulled her mouth away, gasping for breath, but Gina's lips found hers again, drawing her back. Without thinking, Ashleigh parted her legs, allowing Gina's thigh inside. She pressed down hard against her, feeling what she hadn't felt in twenty years—desire and arousal so acute she was afraid she'd climax right then and there. The certainty that she was about to do exactly that pulled her out of her stupor.

157

"Oh, God," she whispered as she pulled out of Gina's arms, her chest heaving as she breathed. She covered her mouth, shocked by what had just occurred. Shocked that she'd allowed herself to lose control so easily.

Gina's face was flushed, her breathing as labored as Ashleigh's. She slowly shook her head. "I'm...I'm sorry."

Ashleigh backed away, her eyes never leaving Gina's. "I have to go," she said in a rush, then quickly fled the room.

She didn't bother with the elevator, instead running to the stairs and pushing the door open. She was surprised that she didn't stumble as she blindly took the stairs down, her mind still reeling. She hurried out, ignoring the receptionist as she passed by. Once inside her car, she leaned back, taking deep breaths, trying to calm down.

"I can't *believe* I just did that," she murmured.

She avoided her eyes in the mirror as she backed up and pulled away from the hotel. The short ten-minute drive to her parents' house passed far too quickly. She wondered if she could sneak up the stairs and into her room without being seen. Even if she could, she knew it would do no good. Courtney would find her.

The house was quiet and she assumed they were still out on the patio. She paused to collect herself, taking a deep breath, hoping she appeared normal as she stepped outside, but only Courtney remained. There was no sign of her parents.

"That was quick."

"Uh-huh," Ashleigh said, eyeing the nearly full bottle of wine. Courtney slid over a glass for her and Ashleigh filled it. "Where are they?" she asked, motioning to the empty chairs.

"Having sex."

Ashleigh nearly choked on her wine. "Gross. Must you?"

"What? You think Mom and Dad don't have sex?"

"I don't want to think about it. And I certainly don't want to talk about it," she added.

Courtney laughed. "Mom told me they bought some sex toys."

Ashleigh sprayed wine on the table as it spewed from her mouth, coughing as some went up her nose. She stared at her sister, then they both broke into a fit of giggles.

"Oh my God," she gasped. "I could have gone the rest of my life without knowing that."

"I know. But now I'm dying to find out what they have."

Ashleigh refilled their glasses. "Why don't you just ask? Knowing Mom, she'd show them to you."

Courtney shuddered and shook her head. "No. I think I'm going to draw the line there when it comes to their sex life. But I think it's great that they're still active."

"Yeah. Great. I mean, it's fabulous to know your parents are having sex and you're not."

Courtney leaned closer. "So what happened with Gina? Did you talk?"

"We said goodbye." She paused. "In her hotel room."

Courtney grinned. "Oh? And?"

"And our goodbye hug turned into a goodbye kiss."

Courtney clapped her hands. "So you told her about Faith?"

"If I'd told her about Faith, I'd be in her bed right now."

"I swear. Isn't that where you want to be?"

Was it? Ashleigh wasn't sure. Yes, she was still attracted to Gina. There was no doubt there. But did she want to sleep with her? Gina was willing, that much was obvious. But what purpose would that serve? She was heading back to Houston, back to her life. Gina would go back to Corpus and do...well, whatever it was she did and whoever it was she did it with. They would still say goodbye.

"Ashleigh?"

"Hmm?"

"Earlier, you said you were afraid."

Ashleigh nodded. "Yes. I'm afraid if I sleep with her, I'll fall for her all over again."

"Ashleigh, you're not a teenager anymore. You're a grown woman. You're allowed to have casual sex and not feel like it has to mean something."

"I know that. But it's different with Gina. It wouldn't be casual."

"How so?"

"For one thing, we have far too much history between us for it to be casual." She took a deep breath and leaned her head back, looking up at the stars. "And I'm way too attracted to her." She rolled her head to the side, smiling at Courtney. "We were fully clothed and standing, and I nearly had an orgasm just from kissing."

Courtney laughed. "Well, yeah, it's been years, right?"

She slapped her sister playfully on the arm. "What I'm trying to say is, one time with her isn't going to be enough. So why torture myself?"

"Torture?"

"My memories of being with her in high school are vivid enough. Why add new, fresher memories to the pile?"

"I think you're taking the wrong approach. She's single. You're single."

"What are you suggesting? That we start dating again?"

"Why not?"

"It would be weird. That's been too many years ago. Besides, we live in completely different cities."

"You could always—"

"No. We couldn't." She shrugged. "And who's to say these feelings aren't just conjured up memories from the past? I mean, just being back here, together, talking about old times, it's bound to have an effect on us, right?"

"I suppose. I just would hate to think that you're letting an opportunity slip away, that's all."

An opportunity, perhaps. But an opportunity for what, Ashleigh didn't know, and she supposed she would never know. She was going back to Houston in the morning.

CHAPTER TWENTY-SEVEN

Present Day

Ashleigh woke from a fitful sleep, the sun sneaking in through the half-closed miniblinds flickering across her face. She rolled onto her back, away from the sun and stared at the ceiling, her mind still on Gina Granbury and that damn kiss, just as it had been each time she'd awakened during the night. She clenched her fists, trying to rid herself of the memory, knowing she never would. How could one kiss have that effect on her? Well, it wasn't really just one kiss, was it? No, it was a heated make-out session, much like those that occurred when they were younger. One kiss always led to so much more. Which is exactly where they were headed last night until Ashleigh came to her senses, thankfully.

Thankfully? Was she really thankful? Instead of waking up alone in her parents' house, she could be in bed with a naked woman. A naked woman whose mouth would be moving across her breasts, waking her slowly. No matter how sated she was, Gina could always arouse her to a state where she was begging for more. Would that be how it could have been this morning? After a night of lovemaking, after they'd fallen into an exhausted slumber, would Gina wake her, wanting more?

"Stop it," she whispered. "Stop it, stop it."

But she couldn't stop it. She wanted to be that woman, that woman in Gina's bed, that woman who would scream with pleasure as Gina made love to her. She remembered it like it was yesterday. The taste of Gina's skin, the feel of those soft hands as they caressed her body, finding all the secret places that only Gina knew. She remembered how it felt to lie on top of Gina, snuggled tight between her legs. She remembered the sounds Gina made when Ashleigh slipped inside her, her fingers finding the spot that would drive Gina wild. And she remembered her own body writhing beneath Gina as she teased her, her mouth getting closer and closer to her center, her tongue finally moving into her wetness, making her climax so hard they would rock the bed.

"Oh, dear *Lord*," she groaned, unable to chase the memories away. They replayed themselves over and over, flashing through her mind with lightning speed. She pushed the covers off and got up, knowing she couldn't just leave and go back to Houston, not like this.

She took a quick shower and dressed, then knocked lightly on Courtney's bedroom door. She smiled as she heard the mumbled "go away," then pushed the door open.

"It's time for you to get up anyway," she said as she sat on the edge of the bed.

Courtney sat up, shoving her hair away from her eyes. "What time is it?"

"Nine."

"You leaving already?"

Ashleigh looked away nervously. "Actually, I'm not leaving."

"Oh? Why?"

"I'm going to see Gina."

Courtney's sleepy eyes opened wider. "You are?"

"Yes. You were right. We need to talk."

"Talk is cheap. You need to have sex."

Ashleigh blushed. "Yes. That too."

"Oh, my *God*," Courtney shrieked. "Are you?"

Ashleigh stood up and smiled at her sister. "Well, if I'm not back by the time you leave, then you'll know how I spent my day."

"You call me," she said as Ashleigh turned away. "I mean it. You call me tonight with details."

Ashleigh laughed. "Have a safe trip, sis. We'll talk soon."

"Tonight," Courtney yelled as Ashleigh shut the door.

CHAPTER TWENTY-EIGHT

Present Day

Gina had just slipped her T-shirt over her head when she heard knocking on her door. She ran her fingers through her damp hair to straighten it, not yet dry from her earlier shower. She glanced at her reflection in the mirror and took a deep breath. Her nerves told her that Ashleigh would be on the other side of the door when she opened it. Was she coming so that they could try their goodbye again in the light of day? No, she doubted that was the case. The way Ashleigh ran from the room last night, she wasn't coming back for another goodbye. Most likely, Ashleigh was angry with her for what happened last night and was here to tell her that. Or maybe she was coming by, thinking Gina owed her an apology.

She paused at the door a second or two, then pulled it open. As she expected, Ashleigh stood there. What was unexpected was the nervousness in Ashleigh's eyes. What? Did she think Gina would throw all etiquette aside and try to resume their rather heated goodbye kiss?

"Good morning," she said, stepping aside so that Ashleigh could enter if she chose.

Ashleigh stuck her hands into the pockets of her shorts, but Gina could still see them fidgeting. "Good morning."

Gina raised her eyebrows, waiting.

Ashleigh offered a slight smile. "I'm kidnapping you for the day."

Gina let the door swing shut as Ashleigh walked past her. "I thought you were leaving today."

"I changed my mind."

"And this is okay with Faith? I mean, that you're kidnapping me and all." Gina stood in front of her. "Does she know about me? About us?"

"Know what?"

"Does she know about last night?" Gina watched as Ashleigh nervously bit her lower lip.

"No. No, she doesn't know anything."

"Okay. Then I'm not going to spend—"

"Oh, so now you're going to turn all chivalrous on me?"

"Ashleigh, if we spend the day together—"

"I know, Gina. After last night, I know."

Gina sighed. They were too old for games between them. "Tell me about Faith."

"Tell you what?"

"Tell me why your mother didn't know she existed. Tell me why both Crissy and Courtney say you're single. Tell me the truth."

Ashleigh plunged both hands into her hair and turned away. "Oh, *God*." She squared her shoulders and turned back around. "Okay. There is no Faith. I made her up."

"Why?"

"Why? Because I was dreading seeing you again, that's why. I assumed you were with someone and I didn't want to appear as some pathetic, lonely woman still pining for you." She smiled slightly. "The fact that I made up a girlfriend in the first place

165

makes me a pathetic, lonely woman, doesn't it?"

Gina was certain she'd never seen Ashleigh looking more vulnerable than she did at that moment. "Are you lonely?" she asked quietly.

"I never thought I was. But after...well, after seeing you again and everything." She nodded. "Yeah, I have been lonely."

Gina took a step closer. "I understand completely how you feel. Last night," she paused, "last night I wanted you in the worst way. You. You ran. I didn't think I'd ever see you again."

"I wanted you too. That's why I ran."

Gina took a deep breath. "Okay. So now what?"

Ashleigh's gaze held hers. "Remember how we used to put a picnic lunch together and sneak out to my grandparents' place?"

Gina smiled. "I remember vividly."

"I thought...well, I thought we could spend the day out there. Maybe hang out at the pool and...and visit."

"Visit, huh?" Gina arched an eyebrow. "Will I need a swimsuit?"

Ashleigh slowly shook her head. "No. You won't need a suit." It was Ashleigh's turn to pause. "So? You want to?"

Gina nodded. "Yes. I want to."

Ashleigh had been blabbing nonstop about the remodeling done on her grandparents' house, realizing she was just making nervous conversation. But really, here they were, heading out of town with the intention of having sex again after twenty years. She figured she was entitled to a little nervousness.

"Ashleigh?"

"Yes?"

"You never used to ramble on so much like this."

Ashleigh laughed. "I'm sorry. I'm not exactly used to premeditated sexual encounters." She glanced at Gina. "Well, not since high school, anyway."

"Can I ask you a personal question?"

"Of course."

"When's the last time you were in a relationship?"

"What constitutes a relationship? I mean, are we talking like together for months? Or years?"

"Either."

"It's been...awhile," she said evasively. Would she really consider anyone she'd dated in the last twenty years as being in a relationship? She went out with Sara for several months, but that was before she learned that Sara was also seeing three other women at the same time. That certainly wouldn't classify as a relationship. She glanced at Gina again. "What about you?"

"No."

"No what?"

"No. I haven't been in a relationship with anyone."

"Not ever?"

"Not since you, no."

Ashleigh was surprised by her answer, but then again, maybe she shouldn't be. Gina hopped around from girl to girl that first semester in college. Maybe that's how she'd spent her life, never settling down with anyone long enough to have a relationship.

Ashleigh slowed, turning onto the road to her grandparents' property. She stopped at the gate, then leaned back in her seat, trying to fish the keys out of her pocket. She held them up and Gina took them. Just like in the old days, Gina grinning mischievously as she got out to open the gate.

I can't believe we're about to have sex.

"Believe it," she whispered. She gripped the steering wheel tighter as she drove through, waiting for Gina to close and lock the gate once more.

When they were young, the gate was never locked and Gina would bound out of the car before Ashleigh had even stopped, hurrying to open it. They would drive through, taking the first dirt path to the left, the road that would lead them to the pond. There, they would lay a blanket on the ground, going through the motions of having a picnic when all they really wanted was to be together and make love.

"Is the old pond still there?" Gina asked when she got back

inside.

"Yes. They actually repaired that old deck and pier. Uncle Dave likes to fish so that was his doing."

They were both silent as Ashleigh drove down the winding road that would take them to the house. When it came into view, Ashleigh was still startled at the difference. It looked nothing like the old ranch house from her grandparents' days.

"Wow."

"I know."

"Did they tear the whole thing down and start over?" Gina asked.

"Once you get inside, you can tell where the old house was. They just added four wings on each side. The modest two-bedroom, one bath is now four bedrooms and five baths. Almost the entire space of the original house is now kitchen and living areas. They sold more than half of the land to pay for the remodeling." They got out, standing at the pristine picket fence surrounding the house. "All four of them now have their own master bedroom, my parents included," Ashleigh explained.

"So when everyone is together for Christmas, your parents stay here?"

"Mostly. Unless all of my cousins come, then they'll give up their room. I mean, it's only thirty minutes from town."

"Is that all? It used to seem like an eternity back in high school."

Ashleigh laughed as she pushed through the gate and went to the front door. "I do believe we entertained ourselves on the drive out." She blushed as she recalled exactly how they entertained themselves.

"Yes. Remember that time when my face got caught in the steering—"

Ashleigh stopped Gina's words with a quick hand to her mouth. Yes, she remembered. She had begged Gina, wanting her mouth, not her fingers, at that particular moment. It was a miracle she hadn't driven them into the ditch. Her jeans and panties were shoved down her thighs, Gina's head was between her legs, and when Ashleigh's orgasm hit, she lifted off the seat with such force, she'd pushed Gina's face into the steering wheel.

She met Gina's eyes, both of them remembering. Then, as it had been that night, they broke into laughter. "Oh, my God. I thought we were going to have a wreck," Ashleigh said as she removed her hand from Gina's mouth.

"I had to brake with my hands."

"I couldn't reach the pedals because your head was—" She stopped, the smile disappearing.

"My head was between your legs," Gina finished for her.

"Yes." Ashleigh's nerves came back full force. Then she smiled. "Technically, your head was now caught in the steering wheel."

She pushed open the front door, about to offer a tour to Gina. When she turned, she knew the tour would have to wait. She'd seen that look in Gina's eyes hundreds of times before.

There was no more need for words. They both knew why they were here. She took Gina's hand, feeling her fingers tighten around her own. She led them down a hallway and into her parents' room. She felt her nervousness subsiding as desire took its place. She stood still, watching Gina, waiting.

"Were you angry at me last night?" Gina asked gently.

"No. If anything, I was angry at myself."

"Because you wanted more?"

"Because I was about to have an orgasm and I was still fully clothed," she whispered. She moved closer, not hesitating as her mouth found Gina's. There was no preliminary exploring. They knew each other far too well for that. Ashleigh gave in to her desires, not shy as her hands traveled a familiar path, moving with a confidence she hadn't displayed in twenty years. Not with a woman, anyway. Just as her hands touched the warm flesh at Gina's sides, Gina pulled her mouth away, her lips nibbling at Ashleigh's throat. Ashleigh lifted her head, granting Gina room as she found the sensitive spot behind her ear.

"*God*, Gina," she groaned, her hands finishing their journey under Gina's shirt. Gina rarely wore a bra and today was no different. Ashleigh's hands cupped her small breasts, loving the feel of rock-hard nipples cutting into her palms.

Their mouths met again in a desperate kiss, both moaning as their tongues battled. Then hands fumbled with shirts and shorts, tangling with each other as they tried to shed clothes. They broke apart, both grinning as they hurried to undress. It was a familiar scene, Ashleigh remembered, as neither of them wanted to stop long enough to get naked.

"Beautiful," Gina whispered. "Always so beautiful."

Ashleigh dropped her bra and reached for Gina again, this time without clothes to block their way. Skin on skin, they moved together, their kisses slower now, exploring, reacquainting themselves to something that was once second nature. And now, like then, their bodies took over, guiding them, leaving no room for thought...or regret.

Ashleigh hastily pulled the comforter back, needing to lie down, needing to feel Gina's weight on her. She tugged Gina with her, a rush of memories sending her senses into overload as her legs parted, letting Gina settle between them.

"Oh, dear *God*," she breathed as Gina's mouth captured a breast, her lips closing tightly over her nipple. Twenty years was too long to go without sexual pleasure and Ashleigh was positive none of the handful of women she'd been with had ever aroused her as much as Gina was doing now. She felt her wetness pooling between her legs and she gripped Gina's hips, pulling her tight against her. "Don't go slow," she murmured. "Not the first time. Don't go slow," she begged.

Gina didn't. She lifted her hips slightly, her hand finding its way between their heated bodies. "So wet," she whispered.

"You always did that to me," Ashleigh replied as their eyes held. She waited, her breath frozen within her as Gina's long fingers filled her. "*Yes*," she hissed, her eyes closing as her hips rose to meet Gina's thrust.

Gina's pelvis rocked against her own hand, forcing her fingers deeper inside with each push. Ashleigh held tight to Gina's waist, guiding her, feeling her power, opening herself fully to Gina. Much too soon, she felt her body losing control, felt herself slipping into the joyous bliss of orgasm. She fought against it, not wanting it to end, not yet.

"Let go," Gina urged as her hips continued to slam into her.

"*God*," Ashleigh groaned, finally giving in, letting herself fall into ecstasy. She gripped Gina's waist tightly, holding her fingers inside as wave after wave of pleasure washed through her. When she opened her eyes, she saw a contented look on Gina's face. "I lied," she said between uneven breaths. "I haven't been in a relationship since you."

Gina's face suddenly turned serious. "I haven't made love to anyone since you," she said, her voice low.

Ashleigh understood what she meant, and the look in her eyes told her Gina was telling the truth. Ashleigh reached up, caressing Gina's cheek softly. "Me either," she admitted. She pulled Gina's head down, her lips lightly brushing Gina's. "I want to make love to you now." She rolled them over, resting her weight on Gina, her mouth moving across her skin. It was all so familiar—her smell, the taste of her skin, the sound of her quiet moans.

"No one's ever made me *want* like this, Ashleigh. Not in all these years."

Ashleigh paused, her mouth inches from Gina's breast. No, she'd never wanted like this either. Never before and probably never again. They would have their fun, then go their separate ways. She squeezed her eyes shut, pushing those thoughts away. None of that mattered now. Not today. Today they would make love, they would be together, they would experience each other's pleasure as adults, not teens. So she closed the distance between them, her tongue raking across Gina's nipple, wetting it before her lips closed around it. Gina always had such sensitive breasts. That hadn't changed, judging by the delightful moans coming from her. Ashleigh took her time, feasting on Gina's breasts, ignoring the urging of Gina's hips as she pressed against her.

"You know, that *don't go slow* works both ways," Gina panted.

Ashleigh smiled against her skin. "Don't be ridiculous," she murmured as her teeth nipped below the swell of Gina's breast.

Gina grabbed one of her hands and tried to force it between

her legs, but Ashleigh resisted. "No. Not that way," she whispered as she moved lower. She couldn't very well tell Gina she had been starving all these years, but right now, she wanted to make love to Gina in the most intimate of ways. As she nibbled along the hollow of Gina's thigh, she felt Gina's hands threading through her hair, pushing her down to where she needed her.

"Ashleigh, *please*," Gina begged. "It's been too long."

"I know," she breathed. *Too long*. She always knew that something was lacking whenever she'd had sex, and she always attributed it to not being in love with the other woman. That may have been part of it, sure. But what was really lacking was that innate connection between two people, a connection that is so natural and instinctive that there's no need for words. Not the spoken word. Not when their souls speak for them.

She raised her head, finding Gina watching her, her eyes dark, filled with desire. No. There was no need for words. She lowered her head, spreading Gina's thighs, moaning at the sight before her. She no longer wanted to go slow. She buried her face between Gina's legs, satisfying a thirst she once thought unquenchable. She held Gina tight as Gina's hips lifted off the bed, her mouth closing over her swollen clit, feeling it throb inside her mouth.

Gina's words were incoherent, one hand still holding fast to Ashleigh's head, the other with sheets tangled in her closed fist. Ashleigh parted her even more, taking all Gina had to offer, her lips tugging, sucking, her own hips rocking against the bed as the taste of Gina ignited her desires. When Gina's hand tightened suddenly in her hair, she used her tongue to send Gina over the edge, loving the deep, satisfied groan Gina made as she held Ashleigh's mouth hard against her.

As soon as Gina's hand went limp, freeing her, Ashleigh slid up, straddling one of Gina's thighs, pressing her hot center hard against her as she sought her own release. Gina's muscles tightened, increasing the friction between them. Ashleigh's breath came in quick gasps as she rode her, her head flung back as she got closer...closer to heaven with each stroke.

But then—seconds before she climaxed—Gina flipped them over. Before Ashleigh could protest, Gina's mouth covered her, her tongue stroking her hard and fast.

"Oh dear...*God...Gina.*" She screamed out, her orgasm blinding her as Gina sucked the very last tremor from her. It was her turn now to hold Gina's mouth against her, slowly coming back down to earth, her hips relaxing, finally releasing Gina.

"I thought I was going to have to kill you there for a minute," she muttered with uneven breaths.

Gina didn't say anything. Instead, her mouth found its way to Ashleigh's breast, slowly nibbling, her tongue snaking out to tease her nipple. Even though Ashleigh's body wasn't that of an insatiable eighteen year old, it still responded to Gina's touch. How, she didn't know, as it was still a throbbing mess of nerves from her last orgasm. But she gave in, not wanting to miss a single second of being with Gina.

"You're as passionate as I remember," Gina whispered against her breast.

"And you're as skilled," Ashleigh replied, her hand moving lazily through Gina's hair as she continued to kiss her breasts.

Gina paused, leaning up on her elbow, watching Ashleigh. "Why are you single?"

"I don't know. I...I used to think it was because I didn't trust anyone."

"Because of me?"

"Yes. But that was really just an excuse. I've had a handful of lovers over the years, but none that got into my heart. And I didn't want to settle for less," Ashleigh admitted. Her hand stilled. "What about you?"

"Honestly? I spent the first ten years running from your ghost. And I've spent the last ten years growing up and accepting ...well, accepting the fact that I'll never find what we had with each other. I don't think it can be duplicated."

Ashleigh nodded. "I know. I've tried to find it too."

Gina returned to Ashleigh's breast, her tongue flicking across her nipple, making Ashleigh moan. "You didn't really pack a picnic lunch, did you?"

Ashleigh shook her head. "No." She tugged Gina up, spreading her legs and urging Gina between them. "Can't you find something else to eat?" she asked wickedly, pulling Gina's mouth to hers.

Gina smiled against her lips. "You may be sorry you asked that question."

"Never."

Gina swam naked in the pool, conscious of Ashleigh's eyes on her. Ashleigh was leaning on her elbow, watching. Her skin glistened, the late afternoon sun touching skin that was normally hidden by a bikini.

"You're still an exhibitionist," Ashleigh said with a smile.

"I'm sure I don't know what you mean," Gina replied as she flipped over onto her back, her breasts now visible above water as she attempted a backstroke. She heard Ashleigh break into a fit of laughter as she sunk below the surface. She came up gasping for breath, joining Ashleigh in her laughter. "Okay, so I don't know the backstroke."

She slicked her hair away from her face, then rubbed her eyes, clearing the water. Ashleigh had rolled over onto her back and Gina was free to stare. After spending hours in bed—until they were both sated and exhausted—they ventured out to the pool, napping on lounge chairs, neither of them bothering with clothes. It had been a wonderful, albeit unexpected, afternoon. After their goodbye at the hotel, Gina doubted she'd ever see Ashleigh again, much less spend the afternoon in bed with her.

But now what? Where did they go from here? Obviously the attraction was still there, even after all these years. As teens, they made love on pure instinct, letting their bodies tell them where to touch, how to touch. Now, as adults, that same instinct took over, their bodies reacquainting, their hands now sure and experienced, no longer filled with wonder. No, making love now had none of the ineptness she felt back then. Even though it was so *good* between them, Gina always wondered if it was good

174

enough for Ashleigh. That insecurity she carried with her was the real cause of their breakup. If she were honest with herself, she would admit that she never really thought Ashleigh was having an affair. But the possibility of one was what drove Gina to end their relationship. Better to deal with a broken heart at nineteen than twenty-five. She shook her head as she realized the absurdity of that rationalization.

She moved back into deeper water, bouncing on her feet to stay afloat. Again, where did they go from here? Was Ashleigh just interested in an afternoon fling? Would they leave here, one going back to Houston, the other to Corpus? Was it premature for her to think that perhaps Ashleigh might be interested in seeing her again? They were both single, neither of them ever finding that one special person to settle down with. Would Ashleigh be receptive to dating?

Gina smiled as she sunk under the water, swimming again into the shallow area. Whatever she and Ashleigh made of things, she doubted they would call it dating. Despite being apart for twenty years, they knew each other too well. Sure, they'd changed some. Everyone did. But the fire between them was still there. Gina suspected it would always be there.

"You actually have the energy to swim?"

Gina shook the water from her hair, standing in waist-deep water. Ashleigh was unabashedly staring at her breasts and Gina felt her nipples harden. "Come join me."

Ashleigh shook her head. "No. You come join me," she said.

"I don't think that lounge chair is big enough."

"True." Her smile was wicked. "I guess I'll have to join you then."

Gina laughed. "Remember that time you almost drowned me?"

"Me? It was you who wanted to try oral sex in a pool," Ashleigh reminded her.

"And I learned that's nearly impossible."

Ashleigh went to the edge of the pool, diving in with barely a splash. She surfaced next to Gina, her hands sliding intimately up her body. "I've had a really good day," she said.

"Me too. I'm glad you kidnapped me."

"I'm starving, you know."

Gina laughed. "So am I."

But their smiles vanished as Ashleigh pulled her closer, her mouth meeting Gina's, urging her lips apart. Gina moaned as Ashleigh's fingers teased her nipples, squeezing them.

"I always loved your breasts," she murmured against Gina's lips.

Gina stood still as Ashleigh's mouth moved lower, her tongue raking across her already rock-hard nipples. Now, as always, Ashleigh's touch chased out all other thoughts. Gina lifted her head to the waning sunlight, her eyes closed as Ashleigh's hand slipped between her thighs.

CHAPTER TWENTY-NINE

Present Day

Ashleigh sat in her car, staring at her parents' house, wondering what she was going to tell her mother. The fact that she was a grown woman who didn't need to explain where or with whom she'd spent the day didn't occur to her. Of course, knowing Courtney, and the fact that there were no messages on her cell, her mother most likely knew exactly how she'd spent her day.

"Just so she doesn't ask questions," she muttered as she finally got out of her car. She paused, letting one last image of a very naked Gina flash through her mind before pushing those thoughts away. She opened the front door, debating whether she should sneak off to her room or find her mother to let her know she was back. The rumbling in her stomach and the very enticing smells coming from the kitchen made up her mind for her.

Her mother glanced at her then motioned to the pitcher of cocktails on the counter. "I won. Thank you very much," she said.

Ashleigh frowned. "Won what?"

"Courtney bet me twenty bucks that you wouldn't show up for dinner."

Ashleigh felt a blush color her face. "I'm so happy I was able to entertain you both," she said as she filled a glass. "I'm starved, by the way."

"No doubt. I trust you left the house in one piece?"

"Oh, good Lord. We went swimming. It's no big deal."

Her mother smiled sweetly. "I suppose you'll let Faith know about your swim party then?"

Ashleigh glared at her. "Are you enjoying yourself?"

"Very much, yes. I assume you did as well."

"If I wasn't so hungry I would leave right now," Ashleigh threatened.

"I doubt it. I made the double battered fried chicken just for you. I figured you'd be ravenous."

Ashleigh's mouth watered at the thought. "And garlic mashed potatoes?" she asked weakly.

"Yes. And homemade dinner rolls."

"You're evil."

"Does that mean you'll stay for dinner?"

Ashleigh pointed her finger at her mother. "But no questions. I mean it."

"But I have a ton of them."

"Sorry."

"You know I'll find out from Courtney."

"As if I'll tell her anything, the big blabbermouth."

After two helpings of everything—and an extra piece of chicken as she was helping her mother clean up—Ashleigh shut her door and fell down on the bed, groaning as she rubbed her full belly. True to her word, her mother had been full of questions, but Ashleigh deflected them all, refusing to answer even the vaguest ones. She'd never been comfortable discussing her private life with her mother. And for the most part, she never really had a sex life to discuss with her.

Today, Gina notwithstanding, she still didn't.

Gina was staying in Calloway until the weekend and she'd asked Ashleigh to stay as well. At the time, Ashleigh had agreed. They could spend tomorrow together. One more day to...to what? Make love? Have sex? Then what? Then Gina would go back to Corpus, out of her life once again. And Ashleigh would be left with fresher, more vibrant memories. Not the stale, used ones she'd carried since high school. One more day of being with Gina. One more day of opening her heart, letting Gina back inside a little.

She rolled over, curling her hands beneath her chin, feeling a familiar ache in her chest, recognizing it as the weight of loneliness she'd carried all these years. By being with Gina, she'd made it worse, not better. As much as she'd enjoyed their time together—and she really, really did—she was just setting herself up for heartbreak all over again. She almost hadn't survived her first broken heart. Now much older, and more emotionally mature, she was still certain she wouldn't survive being hurt by Gina again.

And really, she knew this would happen, didn't she? When she dropped her off, as they said their goodbyes, their hands touching, lingering, their eyes not letting go, she knew. Maybe they both knew that was all there'd be. Just one afternoon. That's all it could be.

Ashleigh had to escape while her heart was still intact. She would leave in the morning, back to Houston, back to her friends ...and back to the job she hated.

Back to the life she hated.

CHAPTER THIRTY

Present Day

Gina hesitated at the door, wondering if she should just leave. Ashleigh's car was gone so obviously she wasn't home. And seeing as it was after one in the afternoon, it should be obvious to her that Ashleigh didn't want to see her today.

She knocked anyway. If nothing else, she would get Ashleigh's cell number from her mother.

Mrs. Pence opened the door with a smile, tugging Gina inside. "I've been expecting you all morning."

Gina frowned. "You have?"

"It's a bit early for cocktails but I have some sweet tea. Will that do?"

Gina nodded and followed her into the kitchen. There was a white envelope on the counter with her name scribbled across it. She looked up, finding Mrs. Pence watching.

"It's from Ashleigh," she said. "Come. Let's go out to the patio." She handed Gina a glass and motioned to the envelope, which Gina snatched up.

"I take it this means she's not here?"

"No. She left early this morning."

Now Gina was really confused. She would have sworn Ashleigh said she was staying until Friday. Gina flipped the envelope over and over in her hands, finally opening it and pulling out the single sheet of paper. Yes, Ashleigh had indeed left. And no, she wasn't interested in seeing Gina again. There was no phone number, no address, no invitation to get together again. Just a *thank you* for a wonderful day, a day Ashleigh attributed to old memories and familiar places clouding their judgment, taking them back in time. A day she would treasure, she said. But it was the last couple of lines that nearly broke Gina's heart.

I doubt we'll ever see each other again. I wish you nothing but happiness.

Gina folded the letter, holding it tightly in her hands. "Wow," she said. "I wasn't expecting that."

"Probably not, no." She pointed to the chair next to her.

"Have you read it?" Gina asked, sitting down.

Mrs. Pence shook her head. "I don't need to read it to know what it says. I know my daughter."

Gina let out a heavy breath. "I guess you know about us then."

"I've never discussed it with Ashleigh, if that's what you mean. Not back then and certainly not now. She wouldn't allow it. But I always suspected, I guess. And when she came home from college, she was so heartbroken, so terribly hurt, I knew it wasn't just some fling she'd had. I knew it was much deeper than that. It all made sense then."

"I'm sorry."

"For what? For hurting my daughter?"

Gina shrugged. "We were kids. We fell in love, only it wasn't a teenage kind of love. It was much more than that."

They were silent for a moment, then Mrs. Pence glanced at her. "I was angry with you at first. We'd opened our house to you, included you in our family. I thought you must have taken advantage of her. It never once occurred to me that Ashleigh was a lesbian." She laughed quietly. "A cheerleader and prom queen. No wonder she hated it so."

"I didn't take advantage of her. It was completely mutual."

"Twenty something years ago. I'm not angry any longer, Gina. Ashleigh's obviously gotten over it. I never thought she would. To see her so distraught, so despondent...well, we were afraid for her. We didn't know anything about having a gay child. You read so much about suicide and all—"

"Oh my God, Ashleigh didn't—"

"No, no. Nothing like that. But she was never the same afterward. Even now, she's still so guarded about things. And not to place blame, Gina. I know there are two sides to every story, but I don't think she's allowed herself to trust anyone again. And certainly not you."

No. Certainly not Gina. She could read between the lines. She knew Ashleigh's letter was just a polite way to say no, she wouldn't take a chance with her heart again. Certainly not with Gina, anyway.

"I don't mean to pry, but I assume you were together yesterday. Perhaps rekindling some old feelings?"

Gina blushed and looked away, only to hear Mrs. Pence laugh quietly beside her. "I'm not an old prude, Gina. I have three very different children. And as closed and guarded as Ashleigh is with her life, Mark is quite the opposite, feeling the need to tell me every detail of his exploits. Besides, if I ran into an old lover who I still had feelings for, I'd most likely spend the day exactly like you did."

"What do you mean, still had feelings for? Did Ashleigh say—"

"No. But she ran away again. It's what she does. If I had to guess, her letter there was thanking you for a good time and wishing you a very happy rest of your life."

"Pretty much, yes."

"You wanted a different outcome?"

Gina stood, feeling embarrassed to be discussing this with

Ashleigh's mother. She paced, her eyes riveted on the pool, the glistening water reminding her of how they'd ended their day yesterday.

"Yes." She turned, meeting her eyes. "Yes. I wanted a different outcome. I thought—however foolishly—that maybe we could see each other, try to start over." She smiled, again embarrassed. "This probably isn't something you want to hear, but the attraction we had in high school is still there. She still takes my breath away."

"I would have to be blind not to see it."

"What do you mean?"

"Gina, dear, when my husband, who rarely has a clue about these things, makes note of it...trust me, it's there. Why else do you think Ashleigh ran?"

Gina held up the letter. "Well, obviously if she feels it, she doesn't want to pursue it. And I don't suppose I blame her."

"Well, I try not to meddle in my children's lives." She smiled. "Never too old to start though. Do you have her cell number?"

Gina shook her head.

"Want it?"

"If you don't mind...yes."

Mrs. Pence laughed. "I've got cell, office, fax. Home address, work address. Her friend Pam's number too. I think I've even got her boss's number somewhere."

Gina smiled. "Thank you. I...I just want a chance. Our breakup way back then was all my fault. It was stupid, childish and without communication. I think . . . well, I think we could have been good together. I think we still can."

"Maybe you should tell that to her, not me."

Gina nodded. "You're right. And I will."

CHAPTER THIRTY-ONE

Twenty years earlier

Gina rolled over to her back, staring at the sky, now turning a pretty orange as the sun faded from view. She would miss this. Even though they'd have more time to be together, she'd miss their quick trips out here. She felt safe here. Just the two of them—no outsiders, no distractions. No one to come between them.

"What are you thinking about?"

Gina turned her head, the thick grass and weeds poking through the blanket against her cheek. She took a deep breath, then turned her gaze back to the sky. "I was thinking how much I'm going to miss this when we leave for college next month."

"What? Sneaking off to my grandparents' place?"

"Yes."

Ashleigh laughed. "I thought you hated having to sneak around."

"The whole concept of it, yes. But this, this is our spot. That tree right there, it's like it's guarding us."

"The fact that we've been coming out here for nearly two years and we've not gotten caught, yeah, it must be guarding us."

Gina rolled over to her side, pulling Ashleigh close against her. "Why do you suppose we've never been caught?"

"Because we pull off the *best friends* thing very, very well. And the *super studious we want to go to college* thing too."

Gina lowered her head, finding Ashleigh's bare breast, loving the quiet moan she heard when her mouth closed over it.

"I love you so much," Ashleigh whispered, her hands now moving across Gina's naked flesh, pulling her closer.

Gina raised her head, finding Ashleigh's eyes, the sunset coloring the air around them. "I'll always love you. You're in my soul."

"And you're in mine."

CHAPTER THIRTY-TWO

Present Day

After washing the few dishes from their lunch, Gina went in search of Aunt Lou. She hadn't actually explained why she was leaving early. And really, it wasn't that she was rushing off to find Ashleigh. She wasn't. She would give Ashleigh some time, give herself some time. But she didn't want to stay in Calloway another day. She wanted to get back home, back to the coast. Smell the salt air, watch the pelicans dive into the surf, listen to the gulls. She wanted—needed—that peace she'd been able to find there. Something she never admitted to before, but the peace she felt was somehow associated with Ashleigh, at the place where they'd discovered their love. She could stand on the beach, watch the waves, and lose herself in long buried memories. Although they wouldn't be so buried anymore. They would be fresh and new and right on the surface...and cut so much deeper than those etched in her teenaged mind.

"What are you doing?" she asked when she found Aunt Lou

standing at a window, staring out into the backyard.

"Oh, I just filled the bird feeder and now those damn black birds are scaring my cardinals away."

"Carly says not to mix the seeds. Grackles aren't crazy about sunflower but they love the mixed seed. Cardinals prefer sunflower."

"Oh, my. Since when did you learn something about birds? Or is this Carly a special friend?"

Gina laughed. "Carly and her partner, Pat, are good friends of mine. Carly's a wildlife biologist. She's taught me a thing or two." Gina sat down on the sofa, waiting for Aunt Lou to join her. "Speaking of special friends, I wanted to share something with you."

"Okay. Is this about a current special friend? I was under the impression you didn't have those."

"I don't date very often, if that's what you mean." Gina leaned back on the sofa, wondering why she felt the need to confess to Aunt Lou about high school, about yesterday, about why she was leaving early. She turned to her. "There's an underlying reason for that but I won't go into all the emotional issues I may have," she said, trying to make light of it. There was no reason for Aunt Lou to know of the horrid reputation she'd had in college—her *whore dog* days, as Tracy referred to them.

"Since you're having a hard time spitting it out, I'll assume it has to do with Ashleigh Pence."

"You know?"

"About high school or yesterday?"

Gina feigned shock. "Why Aunt Lou, do you have spies out and about?"

"Of course not. But you and Ashleigh were inseparable in high school. And when you made it known you were gay and then you and Ashleigh became estranged...well, it was obvious to me."

"Maybe we became estranged because she couldn't handle my being gay," Gina suggested.

"Which would be all well and good had not Ashleigh come

back from college that first term, heartbroken and distraught... and a lesbian."

Gina grinned. "Damn these small towns. Is nothing secret?" Aunt Lou looked away and Gina saw the opening she'd been waiting for all her adult life. "Of course, you had secrets too, didn't you?"

"I don't' know what you mean."

"Oh, come on. I'm not just a curious kid anymore. I'm a full grown woman. And you're not just an old maid who never dated, never married."

"Just because I never married—"

"Aunt Lou, I know what it's like when you have to sneak around to be with someone you love. I did it for two years in high school. And you did it too. Your trips to San Antonio. The *friend* you'd have over for the weekend."

"And you're insinuating what?"

Gina reached over and squeezed her hand. "You know what I'm insinuating. I just don't know why you felt the need to hide that from me. To still hide it. We're kindred spirits in that regard, aren't we?"

Aunt Lou got up suddenly, going back to stare out the window. "Why do you bring this up now? For what purpose?"

"Does there have to be a purpose? Why does our family just sweep things under the rug and never talk about anything? You shouldn't have to go through your life alone. You shouldn't have to hide this part of you."

"You don't understand."

"No. Maybe not. We were a generation apart. Times change."

"Exactly."

Gina stood and went to the window too. "So who was she?" she asked casually.

"It was a long time ago. It doesn't matter."

"Of course it matters. She was someone special to you. Yet you kept her hidden, kept her away. For fear of what, Aunt Lou? Fear your family would turn their back on you?"

"My family, the community, my job. My church." Aunt Lou turned to face her. "Her name was Kathy. When I was younger, I used to go to San Antonio hoping to meet like-minded women. I didn't dare go to a bar though. I took the safe route. There was a feminist bookstore and coffeehouse right at the edge of downtown, before the river became the centerpiece. I met her there."

"And she's the one you'd have over sometimes?"

"Yes. But I was so paranoid, it was hardly enjoyable. I had fears your parents would pop over unexpectedly. Or the neighbors would see her."

"So you locked yourself inside and had wild sex for the weekend?"

"Gina Ann Granbury, I can't believe you said that! Have you no shame?"

Gina laughed at the bright red blush that covered Aunt Lou's face. "I'm sorry. It's what I would have done."

"I don't doubt that, seeing how you disappeared yesterday."

"Ashleigh and I got reacquainted, yes. But she left for Houston today without a word to me. Ran away, really." Gina shrugged. "I guess because of what happened to us in the past, she's got a little fear factor of her own."

"What happened? I know you were awfully young but—"

"We were madly in love," Gina said. "It was my fault. I let my insecurities get the best of me." She waved her hand dismissively. "But that's in the past. What's here, right now, is that Ashleigh is single, I'm single, and we spent a wonderful day together yesterday. A day that, well, that I thought we could build on."

"She doesn't?"

"Well, she left. What does that say?"

"I guess you have two possibilities. One, she's not interested. Or two, she's afraid."

"I don't like the first one. The second is not real pleasing either." Gina held her aunt's gaze. "What about your Kathy? Why did she stop coming around?"

Aunt Lou turned away and Gina thought she wasn't going to

189

answer her. Then she stopped, her voice quiet. "She got tired of waiting on me. She wanted me to move to San Antonio, move in with her."

"Why didn't you?"

"And do what? My life was here, my job, my family. What would I have told people?"

"Who cares? It's your life, not theirs."

"Well I couldn't just up and move without an explanation."

"So you lost someone you loved because you didn't have an explanation to give people? That's just crazy."

Aunt Lou smiled sadly. "I always envied your independent streak, your devil-may-care attitude. I just never had that in me."

"So you let her walk away? How long ago?"

"The last time I saw her was right before your parents divorced." Aunt Lou folded her arms across her chest, her gaze again going out the window. "A long time ago."

"And no one since?"

She shook her head. "I'm sixty-two. I'm past all that."

Gina followed her gaze, landing on the bird feeder, the black grackles fighting for the seed, not a cardinal in sight. "I don't want that to be me," she said quietly. "I don't want to wake up one day and be sixty-two and think it's too late."

"You won't, honey. That's why you're leaving early, isn't it? Because you don't want that to happen to you?"

Gina nodded. "Yes. I'm sorry. I know we didn't really have that much time together."

"Don't be silly. It was good to visit with you. Now, you go after that girl of yours."

Gina kissed her cheek, not wanting to tell her she wasn't going chasing after Ashleigh. Not yet, anyway. Right now, she just wanted to get home, back to the coast. She needed time to sort out her feelings.

"I'll call you," she promised as she headed out the door.

CHAPTER THIRTY-THREE

Present Day

Ashleigh—after much debate with herself on her trip home—decided not to burden Pam and Julie with her exploits during the reunion. Of course, neither Pam nor Julie would consider it a burden. It would be pure entertainment for them. After all, the last they'd spoken, Ashleigh had vowed she hated Gina Granbury and was dreading seeing her at the reunion. To confess she not only enjoyed seeing her again, but that she'd slept with her...well, she just wasn't ready for that scene yet.

No, she took her two bags and headed up the elevator to her apartment. It was still early, the day sunny and hot. She stripped off her clothes, rummaging in her drawers until she found her favorite pair of biking shorts. The black nylon and spandex hugged her body, yet on a very hot and humid day as today, kept her skin dry. Instead of the equally form-fitting and matching shirt, she pulled on a baggy, sleeveless white T-shirt. She twisted her hair and tied it behind her neck, grabbed her helmet and bike and was out the door in less than ten minutes.

She was on her bike for two reasons. One, she'd been a lazy slug for the past week and needed some exercise. And two, she needed to think. The long drive back to Houston would have been the opportune time to sort out her thoughts, but she hadn't been ready to hash it all out. Instead, she'd turned the music up loud, losing herself in mindless lyrics, singing along as the miles carried her farther from Calloway.

And farther from Gina.

Which, in reality, was quite the opposite of what she wanted. She nearly laughed at the absurdity of it all. First, she'd kidnapped Gina for a day of fabulous—really, really fabulous—sex. Then she'd panicked and written her that silly, childish note. And then, as if that wasn't enough to show her immaturity, she ran away.

"Juvenile," she muttered as she pumped harder on the pedals, her thighs straining as she climbed the lone hill on the trail. She relaxed as she crested, the bike rolling easily down the other side. Not only juvenile, but inconsiderate as well. It was almost as if she'd *used* Gina for sex, then left without even a thank you. Especially since she'd all but agreed to stay in Calloway for a couple more days. But no, that wasn't an option. She couldn't see Gina again, she couldn't be with her again. That would only lead to complications, to *drama*. No, she didn't need that in her life. She was perfectly happy—content—just the way things were.

"Liar."

Yeah. Oh, yeah.

She sped up, taking a corner a little too fast but keeping control of her bike. Maybe this trying to get her thoughts sorted out wasn't such a good idea. Because what she knew in her head and what she felt in her heart were two different things. Being the logical person she was now, she decided to go with her head. She'd followed her heart once before where Gina was concerned. Gina had left it broken, shattered. After all this time, it still held the scars.

She squeezed the brakes suddenly, pulling off to the side

of the trail. "What an egotistical bitch you are," she whispered. All this soul searching she was doing was a bit presumptuous, wasn't it? They'd had sex. Great sex. Gina indicated she'd like to spend more time doing the same. Not once did she mention *dating*. Never did Gina suggest they see each other again. Her eyes widened.

And you left her that stupid-ass note.

"Great. Now she thinks I'm an idiot."

CHAPTER THIRTY-FOUR

Present Day

Gina walked alone on the beach, her gaze lingering on the horizon. The morning was surprisingly clear, the water shimmering in the distance as it appeared to be an endless expanse too large for her to comprehend. Seeing the perfectly rounded contours, she found it amazing that long-ago people believed the earth to be flat. Of course, people generally believed what they were told, even if it went against what they thought to be true. It was a trick they used often in their advertising business. If you hear something over and over again, you eventually believe it to be true.

The same could be said for her personal life. However, in Gina's case, it was mostly her telling herself half-truths, ones she'd come to believe over the years. The breakup with Ashleigh was her fault, that wasn't a half-truth. While it was hard to overcome her insecurities at the tender age of eighteen—nineteen—she knew she was using them as a crutch, as an excuse. It was easier than living with the possibility of Ashleigh cheating on her, or worse, Ashleigh leaving her for someone else. Ten years after their breakup she still told herself she wasn't good enough. Not for Ashleigh, not for anyone. So her one-night stands became common practice. No relationship meant no chance of a breakup. Even though she didn't truly believe she wasn't good enough, she'd told herself that so often, for so many years, that she believed it.

Even now, twenty years later, it still nagged at her. Insecurity was no longer the reason for her single status. No, that was attributed to her not meeting anyone who could give her the same feelings that Ashleigh had. She was a confident woman now, a successful business owner. She was content in all aspects of her life. All but one. A week ago, she would have said she was content in her personal life as well. But that was before she'd seen Ashleigh again, before they'd slept together...and before all those long-buried feelings surfaced again. At least for her, they surfaced. But Ashleigh's note conjured up those old insecurities again.

She'd read the note a hundred times. She read the words and she read between the lines. She tried to put herself in Ashleigh's place, tried to imagine what Ashleigh was thinking as she wrote it. Was she running away as her mother suggested? Did she still harbor feelings for Gina? Or was she simply putting an end to it before it ever got started again? Was she afraid Gina wanted to take a chance on their relationship again? Or perhaps afraid Gina *didn't*, and the note was to save face.

Or maybe her old insecurities were true this time. Maybe Ashleigh really wasn't interested. It was a day of sex. Nothing more, nothing less.

She stopped and turned, looking back as the morning sun was now glaring in the sky, heating the summer air around her. The horizon was no longer crisp and clear, the hot, humid air forming the familiar haze that would linger through summer, not lifting until the first cool day of fall. She hoped her own personal haze dissipated much sooner.

"Are you ready to talk about it yet?"

Gina looked up, seeing past the curiosity in Tracy's eyes to the concern. She'd avoided talking about the reunion at all, but she knew Tracy was wondering at her absence each morning this week. She'd taken to leaving well before dawn, making it to the beach in plenty of time to catch the sunrise, to walk the beach, to try and sort out her feelings.

She put her pencil down, the scribbles on the paper resembling nothing more than doodling. The ad she'd been working on for the last two days had yet to take shape.

"I've been a little distant," she admitted. "Sorry."

"A little?" Tracy took the stress ball off her desk and tossed it at Gina. It was a habit they'd taken up from the start, tossing the ball back and forth as they tossed around ideas. Over the years, it had become a symbol of their friendship.

Gina caught the ball, squeezed it between her hands, then tossed it back at Tracy. "I slept with her."

Tracy's eyebrows shot up. "Her who? Ashleigh?"

"Yes."

"Wow. I didn't see that coming."

"Neither did I," she said, catching the ball with one hand. "It wasn't as weird as I thought—seeing her again. In fact, we were able to talk, talk about the breakup, talk about old times."

"And one thing led to another?"

Gina flipped the ball back and grinned. "The dance led to the elevator kiss, which led to the goodbye kiss, which led to the make-out session, which led to Ashleigh taking me away for a day."

"Which led to sex?"

"When we were in high school, we used to sneak off to her grandparents' property. They had this secluded pond with this big giant oak tree. We would go there, take a blanket, have sex." She caught the ball again, then tossed it on her desk, watching it roll to the edge. "We didn't resort to a blanket in the weeds this time. The house is sort of a vacation place for the family now. We had it to ourselves, as well as the pool."

"And you made a day of it?"

"It was a wonderful day. I thought for both of us."

"Oh no." Tracy leaned forward. "One and done?"

"She left the next morning for Houston. Left a note for her mother to give to me."

"Oh, Gina. I'm sorry."

"For what? That she ran out on me?"

"That, yes. I never said anything, but all these years, you've just been going through the motions of dating, not ever really putting much into it. Now, you don't even bother with that anymore. It was because of Ashleigh, wasn't it? You still had feelings for her when you broke up, didn't you?"

Gina nodded. "Yes. I was still in love with her."

"But you were the one who ended things, right? You never really told me why."

Gina took a deep breath. "It doesn't matter. That was twenty years ago." She stood, walking across the office, her hands tucked in the pockets of her shorts. "You're right. I never got over her. Every woman I dated, I compared to her. And no one could ever chase her from my heart." She turned. "I still have feelings for her, Tracy. After all this time, I still do. Part of me thinks she does too." She shrugged. "And part of me thinks she doesn't."

"Well, the only way to find out is to ask her."

"I know. But I'm afraid she'll say no. Then I'll—"

"Be crushed," Tracy finished for her. She got up, coming closer. "Maybe this is for the best, Gina. You need to know one way or the other. If it's no, then maybe you can finally let go of her. Maybe date again, meet someone."

Gina nodded. She knew Tracy was right. But even if Ashleigh's answer was no, Gina would still compare every woman she met, she would still try to recapture that magic she and Ashleigh shared.

And she knew she would fail each and every time.

CHAPTER THIRTY-FIVE

Present Day

"You're bordering on pathetic," Pam said as they walked, not jogged, along the trail.

"So find yourself another workout partner," Ashleigh said.

"You call this a workout? We haven't had a workout in three weeks," Pam complained. "I'll even get on a damn bike for you. Anything but this mindless *walking* we've been doing."

"I think better when I walk."

"It's obviously not working. You've been doing it for three weeks."

Ashleigh stopped, glaring at her friend. "I want to call her."

"Then do it already."

"I'm afraid to. I left that stupid note."

"Stupid-*ass* note," Pam corrected.

"She could call me."

"You didn't give her your number."

Ashleigh rolled her eyes. "Most likely my mother gave her every number I have."

"Why don't you ask your mother?"

"Because then she'll know I want Gina to call."

"And?"

"And what?"

Pam let out an exasperated breath. "You and your mother have a weird relationship. So what if she knows you want Gina to call you?"

"She'll tell me I'm being childish and to call her myself."

"Well you are. And you should."

Ashleigh sighed. "I don't have her number." A lame excuse. She knew all she had to do was call Gina's Aunt Lou. Or even Crissy. But then, they'd know. They'd all know what an *idiot* she was. "Besides, I don't really know that I want to talk to her."

"Okay, just for the record, you're driving me crazy with all this. You just said you wanted to call her."

"No." Ashleigh shrugged. "I need to just let it go. I know that. We had a day together, that's all. It was brought on by old memories, being back there, talking about things. But I know we can't go back, Pam. I *know* that. But still..."

"Look, I can't help you work through this. If it was just sex, then let it go. If it's more, if you still have feelings, then you need to call her."

"No. I will not. First of all, my stupid-ass note indicated that it was just fun and sex, nothing else. I'm not going to make a complete fool of myself by calling her." She shrugged. "And secondly, if *she* still had feelings, then she would have called already."

"Okay, so you've answered my question."

"What question?"

"Whether it was just sex or whether you still had feelings. And yes, you're being an idiot. I thought making up a girlfriend named Faith was absurd, but this is ridiculous. You still have feelings for her. You've *always* had feelings for her. Why do you think you're still single? Why do you think you don't date?"

199

"I told you, there's never been a spark with—"

"Because she's your spark, Ashleigh. That's why you can't find it with anyone else. She's your spark."

It was the truth. There was no need for Ashleigh to pretend it wasn't. "I'm afraid. She shattered my heart, shattered my world. It was so intense with us. I was a kid. I survived. But now, I'm not sure I could."

Pam nodded, apparently understanding. She motioned with her head. "Come on, let's finish our walk."

Ashleigh fell into step beside her, her mind as full of Gina today as it had been three weeks ago. But she wouldn't contact her. She couldn't take a chance. It was better just to let it go and tuck the most recent memories in with the others, only pulling them out on lonely nights...and wondering what could have been.

CHAPTER THIRTY-SIX

Twenty-one years earlier

"Shhh," Ashleigh whispered as the stairs creaked beneath their weight. "They'll hear."

Gina pulled her closer and whispered in her ear. "Hurry. The sun's coming up."

Ashleigh closed her eyes for a moment, the smell of sex still surrounding them. She tightened her grip on Gina's hand, for a second wanting to ditch the sunrise and take her back to bed and make love all over again. But the dawn was approaching, her parents would be up soon, wanting to pack, wanting to get on the road. So she nodded, leading them down the stairs of the rented beach house, careful not to bang the screen door as they hurried out to the deck. She still held on to Gina's hand, pulling her along the trail between the dunes to the beach, slowing finally when they reached the sand. She squeezed Gina's hand hard, pulling her closer now that they were out of sight of the house.

"I hate that we have to leave today."

"I know. And summer will be over before you know it. Then back at school."

"But our senior year." Ashleigh gazed out over the water, the sky still holding on to the night, only a dim flicker of light shown to the east. "One more year, then college. It happened so fast."

Gina led her a little farther down the beach, up against the sand dunes, where they laid out the large beach towel. They sat close together, arms tangled together, the early morning breeze chilling their bare skin.

"Where do you want to live when we get out of college?"

Ashleigh smiled with contentment. She loved it when Gina asked questions like that. It meant they'd be together. It meant Gina *wanted* them to be together. She leaned her head on Gina's shoulder, letting her eyes slip closed as she imagined them older, both dashing off to work after one last hug and kiss, then coming home from work, sharing cooking and dinner, cuddling on the sofa, then in bed, making love, holding each other while they slept.

"Remember last year when I said I wanted to live in a big city?"

"Yes."

"I think I've changed my mind," Ashleigh said. "Nothing small like Calloway though. But I don't think I'd like a big city like Dallas or Houston."

"Austin?"

"Maybe. What do you want?"

"I'd live anywhere with you," Gina said.

"But if you had your choice, where would you pick?"

"I don't know. I kinda like it down here." Gina kissed her forehead, pulling her closer. "The beach, the sand, the surf—it'll always remind me of you, of us. I think even when I'm old, like forty or fifty, it'll still remind me of you and these summers we spent here. It's where we fell in love."

Ashleigh nodded, turning, finding Gina's mouth, their lips moving gently together. "Even if we can't live down here, we should plan to come once a year, just to sit like this, if nothing else."

Gina grinned. "Yeah. Maybe we can still share a house with your parents."

"Funny. No, I want our own place."

"Why? So we don't have to be so quiet in the bedroom?"

"Yes." Ashleigh pulled away, trying to find Gina's eyes in the shadows. "I want to tell them."

"Your parents? Tell them about us?"

"Yes. What do you think?"

"Oh, Ashleigh, I don't know. I mean, they're going to freak out. Your mother is going to freak out. She's still mad that you quit cheerleading. There's the prom coming up. She'll—"

"You don't want me to?"

"I think it could make our last year at school miserable," Gina said.

Ashleigh sighed. "You're probably right. I'm just so tired of sneaking around." And tired of hiding this. She loved Gina. Gina loved her. They shouldn't have to hide it.

"When we get to college, we won't have to. Then we can tell them."

"What about your parents? Do they ever ask you questions?"

Gina shook her head. "No. They don't really seem interested in anything I do. My dad hardly even asks about basketball anymore."

"Do you think you're still going to get a scholarship?"

"I don't know anymore. Calloway is such a small school. We don't really get noticed that much." She shrugged. "It doesn't matter. If I don't get a scholarship, I'll just have to apply for financial aid, get a job. Other kids do it."

"Other kids also have help from their parents."

"I'm sure they'll help me if they can."

"What about your grandmother? The one who paid for Catholic school," Ashleigh suggested. This was one topic Gina never wanted to talk about—paying for college. To Ashleigh, it was the most important thing. She knew she wouldn't have to work. Her parents had already set aside money for her. But Gina? She would struggle.

"If I asked my grandmother, then she'd have control," Gina said. "She'd make me go somewhere else, I'm sure." Gina kissed her. "Don't worry. If it comes down to it, I can always beg my Aunt Lou for help. She doesn't have any kids."

"I'm just scared we're going to end up apart, that's all."

"We'll never end up apart. I promise."

Ashleigh leaned against Gina, both staring across the water as the sun finally showed itself, a giant red orb rising out of the gulf. Around them, the sounds of the day began as gulls swirled overhead and pelicans and herons flew from shore in search of food.

"You swear we'll never be apart?" Ashleigh whispered.

"I swear."

Ashleigh sighed, again resting her head on Gina's shoulder. At that very moment, everything was perfect. Absolutely perfect. Their last sunrise, one she wanted to remember forever. Their last morning at the beach, at least for this year. Gina was right. She didn't think she could ever come down here to the coast without feeling that it was *their* place. Too much had happened between them here. Their first kiss. Their first time making love. And always making plans for their future.

"I love you," Ashleigh murmured. "I mean, I really, really love you."

She closed her eyes as she felt Gina's lips brush her hair, heard her whispered reply.

"I really, really love you."

CHAPTER THIRTY-SEVEN

Present Day

Gina bent over at the waist, trying to catch her breath. She hadn't been on her regular evening run in so long, she felt winded. She also felt good. As good as she'd felt in the last month. The run had taken her focus off Ashleigh, had allowed her thoughts to subside, her mind to rest. After a month of indecision, a month of soul searching, a month of hoping Ashleigh would contact her—she had finally concluded that if anything were to happen, if they were to see each other again, she would have to be the one to make the first move. Ashleigh would not.

She headed slowly back up the beach to the state park where her Jeep was parked, enjoying the evening breeze off the water. The sun had just set, leaving the sky streaked with pinks and reds. She stopped, looking out over waves, a rush of memories coming back to her. She and Ashleigh had been so attuned to each other, the few weeks they'd spent here at the coast were some of the best times of her life. It was the only time they'd been able to be together day and night. They shared secrets, shared their dreams, learned what falling in love felt like. They made promises and talked of the future. And the future was full of so many possibilities. Their future. A future Gina totally screwed up.

She knew she had to get past the what-ifs and what could have been. While they would never get the years back, it would do no good to dwell on them, no good to wish them back. There was also no point in wasting the future years, not if they didn't have to. The only obstacle to that was Ashleigh.

Gina had been over it time and again, trying to figure out exactly what their day of lovemaking had meant to Ashleigh. While it had been playful between them—it always had—there was also an intimacy in their touches, in their glances. Remembering that is what had kept her sane this last month, knowing that Ashleigh had *some* feelings for her.

Now, Gina was ready to find out how strong those feelings were and how much Ashleigh would give her. And how much she would trust her.

The problem was reaching out to Ashleigh. Did she just call her? E-mail? Did she invite her down to the coast for a casual visit? Or did she tell her how she felt and what she wanted? Maybe she shouldn't give Ashleigh a choice. Maybe she should just show up on her doorstep.

She shook her head. No need in trying to force things. She would make the offer for Ashleigh to come down and then let it be her decision. Gina just hoped it was the right decision.

It was nearly dark when she reached her Jeep, yet she lingered, feeling the breeze, smelling the humid air of the gulf. Yes, after all these years, the coast—the sound, the smell, the taste—still made her *feel* Ashleigh. It always would, she knew. She wondered what Ashleigh's reaction would be. Would she still feel that connection?

A thought came to her as she got in her Jeep. She got her cell from the console, finding Pat Ryan's number as she drove away.

CHAPTER THIRTY-EIGHT

Present Day

Ashleigh stared at the box. There was no name on the return address, but even if it hadn't had Corpus Christi there, she would have recognized Gina's handwriting, even after all these years. She left it unopened, instead going to her large windows and staring out over downtown Houston. She wondered why Gina mailed it to her office and not her condo. But the fact that she did confirmed her suspicions that her mother had given Gina all the information she wanted.

But why had it taken her nearly six weeks?

She glanced back at the box, her curiosity piqued. But still, she didn't open it. She was afraid. Afraid of what it was, afraid of what it meant. Was Gina reaching out to her? Why did she wait six weeks? Was Gina afraid too?

She moved closer to her desk, her eyes riveted on the neat handwriting. Gina always had such pretty, elegant handwriting. Must be the artist in her, she mused. She sighed, knowing she had to open it. She found scissors and carefully cut the tape along the edges. The box wasn't large, but it was flat. She hesitated before opening it, aware that her heart was beating just a little too fast. She swallowed nervously, finally breaking the last seal.

She pulled out the bubble-wrapped item, carefully removing the protective plastic barrier. It was a framed print, the 8x10 carefully matted and enclosed in a larger frame. She sat down heavily in her chair, her eyes focused only on the rising sun, the giant red orb coloring the water, the sand, the sun. She blinked several times, her hands trembling as they held the picture.

It was their sunrise.

Oh, Gina.

She took a deep breath, then flipped the frame over. *Pat Ryan Photography*. She nodded, remembering Gina's photographer friend. In the corner was a business card. She plucked it out, seeing Gina's name stenciled across the front. Her address, her phone number. Instinctively, she turned it over. Three words were written on the back.

Come see me.

She dropped the card on her desk and stood up, her feet taking her again to the windows. This time as she looked out she didn't see the endless cityscape of the buildings around her. No, she saw the sun, she felt the sand, she heard the waves, the birds. She closed her eyes, remembering.

She hadn't been back to the coast since that last summer, twenty-one years ago. She hadn't wanted to. At first, the opportunity just never came up. But once she moved to Houston, she was just a stone's throw from the beaches at Galveston. It was then, when she balked at going, that she admitted it was because of the memories the beach held for her. Memories of Gina, memories of them as a couple. And at that time, she didn't want any memories. She still hated Gina fiercely back then and she didn't want any reminders of their relationship. The habit of avoiding the coast, the beaches, became branded in her mind. She never once was tempted to go.

She glanced back at the picture, feeling it beckon her, pull her.

Gina couldn't have found a more appropriate gift, and Ashleigh supposed that was her intention.

Dare she go?

No. That would just be crazy. Because if she went, it would only mean one thing.

Dare I go?

She closed her eyes, remembering the carefree days they shared at the beach. But now, in her mind's eyes, Gina wasn't the teenager she'd been back then. No, she was the woman Ashleigh had made love to after the reunion. She was the woman whose touch still had the power to render Ashleigh defenseless, to make her beg and plead for more, to make her lose control.

She smiled. Teenager or adult, that hadn't changed between them. Their lovemaking was as intense as it had been twenty years ago.

That's what really scared her. The intensity.

CHAPTER THIRTY-NINE

Present Day

"It's going to be so weird," Tracy said as she watched Gina carry another box down the stairs.

"Why weird? I'll still come in to work every day."

"Yeah, but I'm used to you being here when I leave and being here when I get in."

"Well now you'll have that with Darrell."

"I can't believe he wants to move into that tiny apartment." She laughed. "Of course, you lived up there for six years."

Gina added the box to the others by the door. The apartment was tiny, yes, but it had become home to her and she'd grown comfortable there above their office. At the beginning, when they were just getting started, she couldn't afford anything else. Tracy had been telling her for the last several years that she needed to get a real home, but Gina was content living there. It was a bit of a safety net for her. If things didn't work out with the business, she could pack up and leave. Of course, things had worked out.

Their business was steady and Tracy was always adding new clients. She was relatively debt-free. It was time.

Truth was, it was time to get on with her life. It had been over a month since she'd sent the print of the sunrise to Ashleigh. At the time, she told herself she'd give it a week. But when that first week dragged by, she gave it another, thinking—hoping— Ashleigh would call. But who did call was Pat and Carly. They were at the beach house and invited Gina for dinner one evening. Once again, Pat broached the subject of selling. They had been living at the ranch house on the refuge for years and seldom used the beach house. Pat had been trying to get Gina to buy it for the last three years. Gina's excuse was always that she wasn't ready to settle, wasn't ready to commit to that kind of investment. But she was only kidding herself. She *was* settled. This was where she belonged. So this time, when Pat asked, Gina said yes. And that was a whirlwind three weeks ago. Three weeks of securing a loan, dealing with inspectors, insurance, changing over the utilities and hiring a painter. They hadn't officially closed on it yet, but Pat had given her the keys that night. The first thing she needed was furniture. Pat had left a few pieces but most had already been moved to the ranch house. Her old bedroom furniture and the futon, she was leaving for Darrell. Tracy had forced her into shopping one Saturday and Gina had been shocked at the prices. When she suggested a discount furniture store, Tracy told her she was being ridiculous and proceeded to hand her an application for a credit card. Thirty-six months, interest free is what sold Gina, but her debt-free status was disappearing quickly.

"You're taking the rest of the week off. Monday's a holiday. So I'll see you on Tuesday, right?"

"You'll see me on Tuesday."

"Are you sure you don't want to come over on Labor Day? I mean—"

"I know I usually join you guys but I just want to get settled in." She shrugged. "And get used to living there. There's all this space, you know." She pointed up the stairs. "I'm used to that up there, which is about the size of my bedroom now."

"I know. I just worry about you."

"Well quit worrying. I'm fine. And I'm taking your advice and moving on. This is the first step."

Tracy surprised her with a tight hug, one which she returned. "Okay, get out of here. Go enjoy your beach. I'll see you next week."

"I will. Thanks."

Gina picked up the last box then headed out the door. It was still stifling hot but the Jeep was topless. She tucked the box on the trailer she'd rented and pulled the netted cover over everything. She was soon crossing the causeway to Mustang Island. The bay was crowded with fishermen, most getting a head start on the Labor Day weekend. She assumed the beaches would be crowded as well. She was thankful that public access was limited at the beach house. While not considered a private beach, the nearest public access road was two miles away. Most of the beach traffic there would be from other homeowners and their guests.

Homeowner.

She grinned, feeling really good for the first time in awhile. Since she'd mailed the print, that is. She was so sure that Ashleigh would call. Each day that passed brought her down just a little. But now she was moving on. She'd accepted Ashleigh's silence for what it was. She wasn't interested. Fine. Gina wasn't going to force her to talk to her.

So each day she let it go a little more, each day her acceptance of the situation got stronger. She was getting on with her life. Next thing you know, she'd be dating.

She laughed at herself, thinking she must really be getting old. The prospect of dating held none of the excitement as being a first-time homeowner did.

CHAPTER FORTY

Present Day

Ashleigh glanced at her GPS, making sure she was turning on the correct street. She was as nervous as a schoolgirl and twice on the drive down, she'd nearly turned around and abandoned her trip. Of course, logic told her she should have called first. They could have made plans to meet. But so many weeks had passed, she thought it was past the point of being rude. Not only had Gina sent her a beautiful gift—and an expensive one, judging by Pat Ryan's Web Site—but Gina had also extended an invitation. *Come see me.*

And Ashleigh had simply ignored it. No thank you. Nothing. She told herself nothing could ever come of it. She wasn't foolish enough to fall into that trap again. But the scene in the print became too much for her to overcome. It literally drew her in. She found herself staring at it, able to hear the waves, smell the air. If she stared long enough, she was certain to see the rippling of the water, the sun moving higher, the lone pelican in the corner flying away.

Come see me.

Every day it grew stronger—the pull. That invisible string that linked her with Gina, that string that had never been broken. Not when Gina walked away from her, not during their estrangement and certainly not now. It was as strong as ever, pulling at her, beckoning.

It was a week ago that she sat up in bed, her dream so real she could smell Gina, taste her, *feel* her. Her eyes immediately found the print, next to her bed. It was at that moment that she knew she had to go. Not so much the dream, but the fact that she moved the photograph from room to room, from home to office, told her she wanted—*needed*—to go. She'd lose herself for hours, staring at it, imagining them sitting there, watching the sunrise. Imagining so much more.

To say her job had suffered was an understatement. She couldn't muster the enthusiasm for the work any longer. She had written her last loophole, drafted her last contract. She gave them a month's notice, but when they couldn't talk her into staying, not even with a generous pay raise, they terminated her. She wasn't really surprised. It was a cutthroat business and they had their interests to protect.

She wasn't worried. Her savings account was full and would be enough to hold her over without her having to touch her investments. She also knew she wouldn't have trouble finding a job, but she would never go back to the oil and gas industry again. In fact, she was very likely to switch sides. She figured there were many environmental agencies and nonprofit groups who would love her expertise to fight the big oil companies.

But all of that could come later. Right now, she had to find Gina.

She glanced again at the GPS. She was only a few blocks away and she took a deep breath, trying to ignore the anxiety she felt. She remembered the last time she'd suffered from this kind of nervousness—her trip to the reunion. And that time, as well as now, was because she was about to see Gina. She wasn't as apprehensive this time as she'd been then. This time she was flat-out scared.

What if Gina hadn't waited for her? What if Gina had given up on her? Or worse, what if she started dating someone?

No. Gina would wait.

She had to.

Ashleigh pulled into a parking spot, smiling at the name on the wall. *Sunrise Advertising. Sims and Granbury.* It was a beautiful beach scene and she wondered if Gina had designed it. She pushed down her nervousness as she reached for the door, pausing only a second before opening it.

She stopped immediately, thinking perhaps she was in the wrong place. Not only was the office set up haphazardly, but a man and woman were dancing. They stopped, both with startled looks on their faces, then laughter as they pulled apart.

"I'm so sorry. I must be in the wrong place," Ashleigh said, now slightly embarrassed.

"Oh, no, honey. This one thinks she can learn to tango, even though she has two left feet." He sauntered over to her, dramatically placing one hand on his hip and arched what Ashleigh would swear was a perfectly plucked eyebrow. "How may we help you?"

The woman rushed over as well. "Yes, I'm sorry. I'm Tracy Sims." She held out her hand in greeting and Ashleigh shook it. "What can we do for you?"

"I'm actually looking for Gina Granbury," she said. She held up the business card Gina had sent her all those weeks ago. "Is this the right place?"

"Looking for Gina, are you?" His hands switched hips. "I'm Darrell, by the way. And you are?"

"I'm sorry. Ashleigh Pence. Gina and I are—"

"Oh my God. You came."

"Took you long enough," Darrell added before Tracy pushed him out of the way.

"Ignore him. Please, come in," Tracy offered.

215

"Gina's not here?" Ashleigh asked.

"No. She left."

Ashleigh's heart sunk. "Left? For good?"

"Oh, no. No, no," Tracy said. "She used to live here, in the apartment upstairs. She bought a beach house on Mustang Island and she's just moving in this week."

"I see." A beach house on Mustang Island? Was she actually living on their beach? Ashleigh took a deep breath. "I guess I should have called first, but...well, it's been a few weeks since she invited me to come and—"

"You thought she might say no?" Tracy guessed. "And for the record, it's been over five weeks."

"So she's told you—"

"Everything," Darrell supplied.

"Don't you have work to do?" Tracy snapped.

"Oh, now that the good part's coming, you're concerned about my work. You didn't seem to care earlier when you wanted to *tango*," he said.

Ashleigh smiled at their conversation. "It's okay. Maybe I'll just give her a quick call and see if—"

"No, no," Tracy said, smiling wickedly. "I'm going to give you her address and you're going to surprise her."

"But—"

"Oh, this'll be fun. Can we come watch?"

Tracy glared at him then turned back to Ashleigh. "If you'd called, she wouldn't have said no. She's going to kill me for saying this, but she was so heartbroken, so lifeless when she didn't hear back from you. She bought this house on a whim and I'm so glad she did. It's put a light back in her eyes. But you're the one she's been waiting for. All the years I've known her, she's never been interested in anyone. Now I know why."

Ashleigh didn't know what to say. She looked from Tracy to Darrell, then back to Tracy. She didn't know these people and she wasn't willing to share her feelings with them. But to know that Gina was waiting for her—had always been waiting—nearly broke her heart. So many wasted years.

"If you don't think Gina would mind, I'd appreciate you telling me where she is."

"It would be my pleasure."

CHAPTER FORTY-ONE

Present Day

Gina opened up the house, letting in the breeze from the gulf. Even on such a hot day, the breeze made it bearable. Her back was hurting from carrying boxes up the stairs to the beach house raised up on stilts, so she took a break, going out to the deck, her eyes scanning the water, looking at what was essentially her backyard. She was going to love it here. Stepping off the deck for her morning run, evening walks along the beach, watching the stars at night from the deck. Of course, there was one thing missing from that picture, but she didn't want to go there.

Instead, she planned a nice, long weekend alone. She'd get the house in order, set up the huge TV she bought and get the kitchen sorted out. She'd enjoy some holiday traditions like getting the gas grill fired up on the deck, thanks to Pat who insisted it came with the house. She would grill a steak or a burger, enjoy the sand and sun, the beach. She smiled. Yeah, she was going to love it here.

But she still had half a trailer to unload, so she turned away from the water and went back inside.

"Hi."

Gina visibly jumped, then gasped. "Jesus Christ," she said, her hand holding her chest. "What are you doing here?"

Ashleigh shrugged. "You said to come see you."

"Well, it took you long enough." Gina moved closer, not sure if a hug was warranted or not. She motioned at the mess in the room. "Sorry. I'm just moving in."

"I know."

"And I've got the AC off so it's a little warm in here. I was in and out so much, I didn't see the point of having it running." Gina went to the control panel on the wall and turned the AC back on.

"Gina, it's okay." Ashleigh took a step toward her. "I'm sorry I didn't call you."

"You mean after the reunion?"

"That too. I loved your gift."

"Good. I hoped you would." Gina let a little of her hurt show. "Of course, when I didn't hear from you, I assumed the print meant nothing to you and—"

"It means everything to me." Ashleigh reached for her, pulling her closer. "I'm sorry," she said again.

Gina went to her, her arms wrapping tight around her. The feeling of completeness nearly overwhelmed her. "I'm sorry too."

Ashleigh pulled away from her. "You don't have anything to be sorry for."

"Yes, I do. All these years—"

"No," Ashleigh said, stopping her. "No, that's in the past. It's over and done with." She grabbed her hands, squeezing hard. "Can we talk, Gina? Can we just talk? Can we be honest with each other and just...talk?"

Gina nodded. "Okay. I'll start," she said, swallowing down her fear. "I—"

Ashleigh put a finger to her lips, stopping her. "I'll start," she said. "I'll start with why I left Calloway." She took a step back. "One day with you...one day and I fell in love with you all over again. And I left because I didn't want you to hurt me again. I didn't want to spend a few days with you, being with you, making love with you then have you leave me. I just couldn't do it. So—"

"So you left me instead," Gina finished for her. "At first, I thought it was a payback for twenty years ago."

"No. I would never do that to you. But I thought maybe you'd call, maybe it meant something to you too."

Gina motioned out to the deck and Ashleigh followed her. The afternoon sun had shifted, offering them shade on the deck. *I fell in love with you all over again.* Was it true? Could one day together erase the betrayal, the hatred, the anger?

"It did mean something to me," Gina admitted. "That's why I was so surprised when you left. I must have read your note a hundred times," Gina said. "That's why I didn't call. Sometimes I'd read it and I thought maybe you wanted me to call." She shrugged. "And other times, it would sound so final. I didn't want to contact you if you had no desire to see me," she said.

"It was stupid of me to leave the note," Ashleigh said. "And then I felt silly for leaving it, presuming you wanted to see me and trying to cut you off, yet not knowing if you even *wanted* to see me in the first place."

"I go to the state park on the island," Gina said. "I used to go there to run. It was always so peaceful for me, comforting. I never realized it before, but it was where I felt you. After the reunion, when I went out there, it hit me. The years I'd been living here, that's why I gravitated to the beach. It made me feel close to you, a part of you. Or maybe you a part of me, I don't know." Gina took her hand, letting their fingers entwine. "One evening, right at sunset, the sky was full of colors, the day was ending and I was thinking about you. I didn't want to let another day go by without reaching out to you, yet I didn't want to just call. I didn't want to force you to talk to me if you didn't want to. I felt so connected to you here, I thought maybe you'd feel it too. So I went to Pat's gallery in Rockport. I saw that print and I knew it was the one. A beautiful sunrise, the beginning of a new day. Maybe a new life."

"Oh, Gina. I'm sorry it took me so long to come. I was just so scared. I needed to—"

"I love you, Ashleigh. I've *always* loved you."

Their eyes held for long seconds, neither pulling away. In those blue depths, Gina saw the uncertainty fade away, the doubt melt. She waited, finally seeing what she needed to see. Ashleigh moved into her arms.

"Tell me again."

Gina kissed her slowly, without the urgency she'd felt the last time. "I love you," she whispered against her lips. She pulled Ashleigh tighter into her arms, into her heart, into her soul. She would never let her go again.

"Perhaps we should go inside," Ashleigh suggested when their kisses turned heated. "I would love a tour of the house."

"A tour? Sure." Gina closed the door behind them, then held her hands out. "Living room." She pointed. "Kitchen. The utility room is—"

"I want to see your bedroom," Ashleigh said, her voice low. "I'd really, really like to see your bedroom."

"I see." Gina took a step closer to her. "So the tour was only a ploy?"

"Yes."

"Imagine that."

Ashleigh closed the distance between them. "We should probably talk first, but I just want to be with you." Her hands moved under Gina's T-shirt, finding her braless. "I swear, do you *ever* wear a bra?"

Gina sucked in her breath as Ashleigh's hands closed over her breasts. "No. I'm not sure they make bras that small," she said before Ashleigh's mouth found hers.

"They're prefect," Ashleigh murmured. She leaned her head back, meeting Gina's eyes. "I love you. I don't want to be apart any longer."

Gina nodded. "Me either. Houston's not that far away. I could always—"

"No. We belong together *here*," Ashleigh said. "Besides, I kinda quit my job."

Gina raised her eyebrows. "So...you're kinda free then?"

"Kinda, yeah."

"So you can stay with me all weekend?"

"Yes."

It struck Gina suddenly. Here they were, calmly discussing their future, acting like it hadn't been two and a half months since the reunion. But then, it had always been like that between them. After twenty years of being separated, they'd picked up right where they left off, reconnecting, letting nature takes its course for them. Both of them should have known not to fight it.

She smiled, pulling Ashleigh's hands from under her shirt. "I love how we do this."

"Do what?"

"Just pick right up as if nothing's happened."

"I'm sorry. I just—"

"No, Ashleigh. I meant that sincerely. We could draw this out with lots of drama, but why? We both know we belong together. We're connected," she said, pointing to her heart. "We always have been."

"Yes."

"This is what I've always wanted. A life with you. The last twenty years have been so damn empty. We can't get them back, but I hope we can make up for the loss." She took a deep breath. "I've loved you all these years, Ashleigh. I promise to love you until I die."

Ashleigh's eyes filled with tears. "And I promise to always be with you. I give you my heart, my soul . . . my life. I give you my love."

Gina leaned closer, lightly brushing her lips. "Did we just get married?"

Ashleigh laughed as she wiped at her tears. "If we did, then I'm ready for the wedding night."

"I'm ready too." Gina took her hand, leading her down the short hallway to the bedroom. She paused at the door. "Our bedroom."

Ashleigh stepped into the room, her gaze traveling over the new furniture, the polished hardwood floors and new rug, to the four large windows providing an endless view of the Gulf of Mexico. She slowly turned back to Gina.

"It's gorgeous. Everything is so beautiful."

"I'm glad you like it. If you want different furniture, we can always—"

"Oh, no. This is lovely. It's perfect here."

Gina nodded, pleased she liked it. But she felt they'd done enough talking. She pulled her shirt over her head, watching as Ashleigh's gaze traveled to her breasts. Ashleigh walked closer, then stopped. She slowly pulled her own T-shirt off, her fiery eyes never leaving Gina's as she disposed of her bra as well.

"I've never seen a woman more beautiful than you, Ashleigh," Gina whispered.

"Gina, you, my darling, are a goddess. And I'm going to make love to you and show you how much I truly love you," she said, her hands sliding over Gina's shoulders and pulling them together. She paused, their lips only an inch apart. "You're mine, Gina. I'll never let you go again."

Gina lowered her head, their lips meeting, mouths opening to each other. Gina led her to the bed, pulling Ashleigh down with her. True to her word, Ashleigh took control, kissing Gina with such passion, she nearly whimpered. She wanted to tell Ashleigh to hurry, but the look in her eyes told Gina it would be a slow, glorious torture—her lovemaking. She gave in to the hands and mouth moving over her body, relinquishing the power to Ashleigh.

There was no need to hurry. They had the rest of their lives to love each other.

CHAPTER FORTY-TWO

Present Day

"Come on, get up."

Ashleigh groaned and rolled over, seeing nothing but darkness outside the windows. "You're kidding, right?" she mumbled.

"No. I want to show you something."

"Gina, please. We just went to sleep. I'm exhausted."

"I know. I was up with you, remember?"

Ashleigh opened her eyes again. "How can you be so chipper? We've had maybe two hours of sleep."

"You're the one who kept waking me up so that you could—"

Ashleigh covered Gina's mouth with her hand. She knew perfectly well what she had done. And the thought of it aroused her again, despite her exhaustion. She reached for Gina, trying to pull her down to her but Gina resisted.

"Oh no you don't," Gina said, standing up again. "Up. You've got to see this."

Ashleigh groaned again and sat up, rubbing her eyes. Her

stomach rumbled. "Did we even eat last night?"

"No."

"No wonder I'm starving. Are you trying to kill me?"

"Me? You're the one—"

"Okay, okay," Ashleigh said, holding her hand up, stopping her. "So I got a little crazy last night. It was just so perfect, and it felt so good to be with you."

"Ashleigh, we can't make up for twenty years in one night. We'll kill each other."

Ashleigh smiled, watching as Gina's gaze drifted to the windows. The night sky was showing signs of light. Dawn.

Gina turned back to her. "We need to hurry."

Finally Ashleigh understood. The sunrise. She nodded. "Okay." She slipped into the shorts she'd discarded hours and hours ago then blindly put on a T-shirt that she immediately recognized as being Gina's.

"Looks good on you."

Ashleigh followed Gina into the living room. "Coffee?" she asked hopefully.

"Yep."

Two mugs sat on the counter and Gina filled them. She searched through an unpacked box, pulling out a bag of brown sugar. "Will this do?"

"Perfect."

"You don't do cream, right?"

"Right."

"Good. Because I don't have any. I haven't done any shopping yet."

"We can go together," Ashleigh offered. She sipped from her coffee with a satisfied moan.

"Come on. I promise to take you out to breakfast later."

They went out the back and down the stairs to the sand. Gina had a towel tucked under her arm and she led Ashleigh closer to the water. Gina stopped, looking back at the beach house, silently counting.

"What are you doing?"

"You'll see."

She walked three paces to the east, then handed Ashleigh her coffee cup so she could lay the towel out. They sat side-by-side, quietly sipping their hot coffee, waiting for the day to come alive.

Ashleigh leaned her head on Gina's shoulder, feeling total and utter contentment. Which, considering the last couple of months of turmoil, was a huge change. Gina was right. She had been trying to make up for twenty years last night. It just felt so good to be together. So right. There was no apprehension, no fear or dread. No concern as to what tomorrow would bring. They were together. There would be no games between them. They made a pact last night that no matter what happens, they would talk. They would communicate. They would build a life together.

"Listen," Gina whispered.

Ashleigh did, finally hearing the first stirrings of the birds. Gulls off in the distance, the distinctive call of a heron as it flew out into the bay, the tiny chirps of the shorebirds as they returned for their morning meal, sounds she remembered from so long ago. She followed Gina's gaze as the first colors of the morning began painting the sky—the softest of pinks before a darker red appeared.

She put her coffee cup down, snuggling closer to Gina as the sun rose out of the water, the giant orb turning the sky a beautiful crimson, the colors streaking out in all directions. The sky, the water, all bursting in reds and oranges. She absorbed it all, taking it in, shocked by the familiarity of it. It had been twenty-one years since she'd sat on the beach and watched a sunrise, yet it felt like only yesterday. She sat up straighter, her eyes widening.

"Oh my God," she whispered.

"Do you see it now?"

"This is...this is the picture," she said, knowing it was true. She'd stared at this scene for hours on end, this beach, this sunrise.

"Yes. Pat told me she took that shot right here. It's the main reason I bought the house. I thought maybe, even if you weren't here with me, maybe you'd look at that picture occasionally. And you'd be looking at what I was looking at."

"Oh, Gina. That's so romantic. That picture was the perfect thing to send me. I stared at it constantly. The picture became you. I took it with me everywhere. To work, back home again. I slept with it beside my bed. It was my connection to you."

Gina leaned closer and kissed her lightly. "It's right here. I'm right here."

Yes, Gina was right here, in her arms. Where Ashleigh vowed she would always be.

"I love you, Gina. Always."

"I love you. You're the light in my life. The light that's been missing." She kissed her again then stood, pulling Ashleigh to her feet. "I promised you breakfast," she said.

"After that beautiful, romantic sunrise, you want to have breakfast? I was thinking more like breakfast in bed."

"You said you were starving," Gina reminded her as they walked back to the house.

"Well, that's true."

"Breakfast. Shopping. Unpacking."

"Unpacking?"

"Yeah. Because if we go shopping and unpack the kitchen boxes, then we won't have to go out again." She wiggled her eyebrows teasingly. "That would mean breakfast in bed."

Ashleigh stood on the bottom step, making her taller than Gina. She pulled her closer, kissing her thoroughly. "I can't believe how everything worked out," she said. "It's almost too perfect."

"I think we deserve it. We've been so long without love."

Ashleigh touched her face, caressing her skin gently. "I'm glad you waited."

"There was no choice. There's never been anyone but you, Ashleigh. I'd have waited the rest of my life."

Ashleigh nodded. "Yes. I would have too." She kissed her again. "Take me to breakfast now or I'm taking you to bed," she murmured against her lips.

Gina wrapped her arms around Ashleigh, lifting her off the stairs and turning her in a circle, causing Ashleigh to laugh with joy as she held on tight. Gina set her down and slipped her hands under Ashleigh's T-shirt. Desire replaced hunger immediately.

"Breakfast can wait, hmmm?" Gina asked, staring into Ashleigh's eyes as her hands covered her breasts.

Ashleigh nodded. "Oh, yeah." She moved closer, pressing her body to Gina's. "Breakfast can wait. Love can't."

They broke apart, hurrying up the stairs and into their new life. Together.

Publications from Bella Books, Inc.
Women. Books. Even better together
P.O. Box 10543 Tallahassee, FL 32302 Phone: 800-729-4992
www.bellabooks.com

TWO WEEKS IN AUGUST by Nat Burns. Her return to Chincoteague Island is a delight to Nina Christie until she gets her dose of Hazy Duncan's renown ill-humor. She's not going to let it bother her, though...
978-1-59493-173-4 $14.95

MILES TO GO by Amy Dawson Robertson. Rennie Vogel has finally earned a spot at CT3. All too soon she finds herself abandoned behind enemy lines, miles from safety and forced to do the one thing she never has before: trust another woman.
978-1-59493-174-1 $14.95

PHOTOGRAPHS OF CLAUDIA by KG MacGregor. To photographer Leo Wescott models are light and shadow realized on film. Until Claudia.
978-1-59493-168-0 $14.95

SONGS WITHOUT WORDS by Robbi McCoy. Harper Sheridan runaway niece turns up in the one place least expected and Harper confronts the woman from the summer that has shaped her entire life since.
978-1-59493-166-6 $14.95

YOURS FOR THE ASKING by Kenna White. Lauren Roberts is tired of being the steady, reliable one. When Gaylin Hart blows into her life, she decides to act, only to find once again that her younger sister wants the same woman.
978-1-59493-163-5 $14.95

THE SCORPION by Gerri Hill. Cold cases are what make reporter Marty Edwards tick. When her latest proves to be far from cold, she still doesn't want Detective Kristen Bailey baby-sitting her, not even when she has to run for her life.
978-1-59493-162-8 $14.95

STEPPING STONE by Karin Kallmaker. Selena Ryan's heart was shredded by an actress, and she swears she will never, ever be involved with one again.
978-1-59493-160-4 $14.95

FAINT PRAISE by Ellen Hart. When a famous TV personality leaps to his death, Jane Lawless agrees to help a friend with inquiries, drawing the attention of a ruthless killer. #6 in this award-winning series.
978-1-59493-164-2 $14.95

A SMALL SACRIFICE by Ellen Hart. A harmless reunion of friends is anything but, and Cordelia Thorn calls friend Jane Lawless with a desperate plea for help. Lammy winner for Best Mystery. #5 in this award-winning series.
978-1-59493-165-9 $14.95

NO RULES OF ENGAGEMENT by Tracey Richardson. A war zone attraction is of no use to Major Logan Sharp. She can't wait for Jillian Knight to go back to the other side of the world.
978-1-59493-159-8 $14.95

TOASTED by Josie Gordon. Mayhem erupts when a culinary road show stops in tiny Middelburg, and for some reason everyone thinks Lonnie Squires ought to fix it. Follow-up to Lammy mystery winner Whacked.
978-1-59493-157-4 $14.95

SEA LEGS by KG MacGregor. Kelly is happy to help Natalie make Didi jealous, sure, it's all pretend. Maybe. Even the captain doesn't know where this comic cruse will end.
978-1-59493-158-1 $14.95

KEILE'S CHANCE by Dillon Watson. A routine day in the park turns into the chance of a lifetime, if Keile Griffen can find the courage to risk it all for a pair of big brown eyes.
978-1-59493-156-7 $14.95

ROOT OF PASSION by Ann Roberts. Grace Owens knows a fake when she sees it, and the potion her best friend promises will fix her love life is a fake. But what if she wishes it weren't?
978-1-59493-155-0 $14.95

COMFORTABLE DISTANCE by Kenna White. Summer on Puget Sound ought to be relaxing for Dana Robbins, but Dr. Jamie Hughes is far too close for comfort.
978-1-59493-152-9 $14.95

DELUSIONAL by Terri Breneman. In her search for a killer, Toni Barston discovers that sometimes everything is exactly the way it seems, and then it gets worse.
978-1-59493-151-2 $14.95

FAMILY AFFAIR by Saxon Bennett. An oops at the gynecologist has Chase Banter finally trying to grow up. She has nine whole months to pull it off.
978-1-59493-150-5 $14.95

SMALL PACKAGES by KG MacGregor. With Lily away from home, Anna Kaklis is alone with her worst nightmare: a toddler. Book Three of the Shaken Series.
978-1-59493-149-9 $14.95

WRONG TURNS by Jackie Calhoun. Callie Callahan's latest wrong turn turns out well. She meets Vicki Brownwell. Sparks would fly if only Meg Klein would leave them alone!
978-1-59493-148-2 $14.95

WARMING TREND by Karin Kallmaker. Everybody was convinced she had committed a shocking academic theft, so Anidyr Bycall ran a long, long way. Going back to her beloved Alaskan home, and the coldness in Eve Cambra's eyes isn't going to be easy.
978-1-59493-146-8 $14.95